'You are under my employ as a fill-in housekeeper,' he said. 'Don't go getting any ideas of filling in other areas of my life.'

She gave him a withering look. 'You would have to pay me a king's ransom to become your latest mistress,' she said.

Alessandro felt his lower spine zap with searing heat. 'Dangerous words, Rachel,' he warned silkily. 'Don't go throwing challenges down at me like that. I might just take you up on it.'

Rachel glared at him. 'People like you think you can buy anything you want, don't you? But I am not selling myself—and certainly not to you.'

'Sleeping rough not your thing any more, little rich girl?' he asked, with a mocking slant to his mouth.

She ground her teeth. 'I am offering to work as your housekeeper. Nothing else.'

Melanie Milburne says: 'I am married to a surgeon, Steve, and have two gorgeous sons, Paul and Phil. I live in Hobart, Tasmania, where I enjoy an active life as a long-distance runner and a nationally ranked top ten Master's swimmer. I also have a Master's Degree in Education, but my children totally turned me off the idea of teaching! When not running or swimming I write, and when I'm not doing all of the above I'm reading. And if someone could invent a way for me to read during a four-kilometre swim I'd be even happier!'

Recent titles by the same author:

THE WEDDING CHARADE*
SHOCK: ONE-NIGHT HEIR*
SCANDAL: UNCLAIMED LOVE-CHILD*
THE MÉLENDEZ FORGOTTEN MARRIAGE

The Sabbatini Brothers

Did you know that Melanie also writes for Mills & Boon® Medical ™ Romance?

HIS POOR LITTLE RICH GIRL

BY
MELANIE MILBURNE

MILLS & BOON

First published in Great Britain 2011
by Mills & Boon, an imprint of Harlequin (UK) Limited,
Eton House, 18-24 Paradise Road, Richmond, Surrey TW9 1SR

© Melanie Milburne 2011

ISBN: 978 0 263 88687 0

Harlequin (UK) policy is to use papers that are natural, renewable and recyclable products and made from wood grown in sustainable forests. The logging and manufacturing process conform to the legal environmental regulations of the country of origin.

Printed and bound in Spain
by Blackprint CPI, Barcelona

HIS POOR LITTLE RICH GIRL

CHAPTER ONE

RACHEL had waited for over an hour to meet with the proposed financial backer of her fashion label. She still hadn't quite got in front of the jet lag and had to fight to keep her eyes open on the magazine she was leafing through as she waited in the plush reception area.

At last she was led through to the corporate executive's office by his receptionist on legs that felt woolly with excitement.

This is it, she thought as she walked through the door. *I won't have to lose everything I have worked so hard for.*

'I am sorry, Ms McCulloch,' the late middle-aged corporate executive said with an apologetic smile even before Rachel could take a seat. 'We have changed our mind. Our company is undergoing some restructuring. We are not prepared to take a risk on such a relatively unknown designer as you. You will have to go elsewhere for the financial backing you require. We are no longer interested.'

Rachel blinked at the older man in shock. 'Not interested?' she choked. 'But I thought… Your letter said… But I've come all this way!'

He held up a hand as if directing the heavy traffic that rumbled over the cobbled streets of Milan outside. 'We have been advised against it by a highly respected business analysis expert,' he said. 'The board has made its final decision. I suggest you consider other options for finance.'

Other options? What other options? Rachel thought in gut-twisting despair. She had to get her evening wear label launched in Europe. Everything she had worked for, all the sacrifices she had made, all the heartache and hard work surely couldn't end like this. She would look a fool all over again if this failed. If she didn't get this money the company would go into receivership. She needed money and she needed it quickly.

She could *not* fail.

Rachel frowned as she addressed the executive. 'Who exactly advised against backing me?'

'I am sorry but I am unable to divulge that information,' he said.

She felt her spine go rigid, suspicion crawling over her skin like a long-legged insect. 'You said it was a highly respected business analysis expert.'

'That is correct.'

'Would that be Alessandro Vallini by any chance?' she asked with a pointed look.

'I am sorry, Miss McCulloch,' he said. 'I am not at liberty to confirm or deny anything.'

She stood up, hoisting her handbag over her shoulder with grim determination. 'Thank you for your time,' she said curtly and left.

Rachel found the address of Alessandro Vallini's Milan office on the search engine on her phone. It was a gracious-looking building, old but classy and stylish, signifying the success of the man behind the business. It was a stellar rise to the top. As self-made men went, he surely was an outstanding example of how far one could go irrespective of a disadvantageous background. Seeing him face to face was not something she had originally planned to do, but clearly he had engineered this so she would track him down.

'I would like to see Signor Vallini,' Rachel said without preamble to the smartly dressed receptionist behind the desk.

'I am sorry but Signor Vallini is currently taking an extended summer break at his villa in Positano,' the receptionist said. 'He is conducting all his business from there.'

'Then I would like to make an appointment to see him at the earliest opportunity,' Rachel said.

'Are you an existing client?' the receptionist asked.

'No, but I—'

'I am sorry but Signor Vallini is not taking on any new clients until after he returns from his break,' the receptionist said. 'I could schedule something for you in late September, perhaps?'

Rachel frowned. 'But that's more than a month away. I'm only here until the end of the August.'

'I am sorry but—'

'Look, I'm not really a client,' Rachel said, hoping she could pull off the little white lie. 'I'm a…an old friend of his from Melbourne. He used to work for my father. I was hoping we could catch up while I am here. My name is Rachel McCulloch.'

There was a slight pause.

'I will have to speak to him first,' the receptionist said, and, picking up the receiver, added, 'If you wouldn't mind taking a seat over there?'

Rachel sat on one of the butter-soft leather sofas, trying not to think of the last time she had seen Alessandro. If her instincts were right and he had been the one to sabotage her attempt to gain financial backing it proved one thing clearly: he still hadn't forgiven her.

'I am sorry but Signor Vallini does not wish to see you,' the receptionist said.

Rachel shot to her feet. 'But I must see him,' she insisted. 'I absolutely must see him.'

'I am under strict instructions to inform you that under no circumstances will Signor Vallini agree to see you,' the receptionist said.

Rachel was outraged. He was obviously playing with her. Did he really think she would take no for an answer after what he had just done? As paybacks went it was certainly an effective one but she wasn't going to allow him to get away with it. Of course he would see her.

She would *make* him see her.

Rachel's stomach dipped and dived all the way down the Amalfi coast road leading towards Positano, but it had little to do with the hair-raising twists and bends the bus wove around. She had planned to hire a car but her credit card had been declined at the booking counter. It had been an embarrassing experience, one she was unlikely to forget in a hurry. The phone call to her bank back in Australia had given her little comfort. It seemed a red flag had come up on her account and it would take at least twenty-four hours to clear it given her financial history after Craig had forged her name on various loans three years ago. She needed money more than ever and she needed it now.

The bus dropped her at the foot of the road that led to the Villa Vallini set high on the cliff. But when the driver opened the luggage compartment to locate her one bag it was nowhere to be seen.

'It must have been put on one of the other buses,' the driver said, closing the compartment.

'How could that have happened?' Rachel asked, trying not to panic.

He shrugged. 'It happens now and again. I will contact head office and make sure it is delivered to your hotel. If you give me your details I will see to it.' He took out a pen and a clipboard.

'I haven't actually booked a hotel as yet,' Rachel said, chewing at her lip as she thought of her current lack of funds.

'Just give me your mobile phone number then and I will call you when we locate the bag,' he said.

Rachel stood on the roadside as the bus finally pulled away, and then her eyes went to the villa above her. The magnificent private residence was set slightly apart from its neighbours. It was centuries old, built on four levels, with luxurious terraced gardens and an infinity pool that was set high above the ocean. The sun sparkled off the brilliant blue water invitingly, making each bead of perspiration rolling down between Rachel's shoulder blades all the more unbearable. The sun pierced her eyeballs like dressmaking pins, and the vague headache she had been fighting all day now started to inflict hammer blows of pain around her temples.

She garnered her determination and trudged on up the long steep steps that led to the imposing front gates of the villa. The double gates were locked and so too was the side gate for foot traffic. There was however an intercom button that was set in the stone wall beside the ornate shiny black and gold gates.

'Non ci sono visitatori,' a woman said before Rachel could say a word.

Rachel leaned closer to the speaker. 'But I—'

The intercom went dead. She looked up at the villa, wincing as the sunlight stabbed again at her eyes. She clutched at the wrought iron of the gates and took a couple of deep breaths before she pressed the buzzer again.

The woman answered again, this time in heavily accented English. 'No visitors.'

'I have to see Alessandro Vallini,' Rachel said. 'I am not leaving until I do.'

'Please go away,' the woman said.

'But I have nowhere else to go,' Rachel said, almost to the point of begging. 'Could you please tell Signor Vallini that? I have nowhere else to go.'

The intercom went dead again and Rachel turned her back against the hot stone and slid down to sit in a patch of shade. She lowered her head to her bent knees, unable to believe this was happening to her. It was as if she had stepped into someone else's life. She had grown up with money, lots of money, more money than most people saw in a lifetime. For so long she had taken it for granted. She had wanted for nothing and had not for a moment thought it could all be taken away. But it had been, and, although she had worked hard to rebuild her life over the last couple of years, now she was reduced to begging at the gates of the man she had walked away from five years ago. Was this karma? Was this how fate had decided to play things? She closed her eyes and prayed for the pain in her head to ease. Then she would get up and try again and again until Alessandro finally agreed to see her...

'Is she still there?' Alessandro asked his housekeeper Lucia.

'*Sì, signor,*' Lucia said, turning from the window. 'It has been over an hour. It is very hot out there.'

Alessandro rubbed at the tense spot in his jaw as he fought

with his conscience. He was locked away in his tower while Rachel was down there in the boiling heat but his gut clenched with the dread of her seeing him like this. He hadn't expected her to arrive unannounced. He had already had his secretary refuse her an appointment. He had hoped that would be enough to put her off. How long until she gave up and went away? Why wasn't she getting the message? He didn't want to see her. He didn't want to see anyone.

'*Mon Dio*, I think she is going to faint!' Lucia said grabbing at the window sill with both hands.

'It is probably an act,' Alessandro said calmly, turning back to the papers on his desk, doing his best to ignore the two flick knives of guilt and anguish inside his stomach.

Lucia frowned as she stepped away from the window. 'Perhaps I should take her some water to see if she is all right.'

'Do what you like,' he said, flipping a page of the document he had lost interest in half an hour ago. 'Just keep her away from me.'

'*Sì, signor,*'

Rachel opened her eyes to see an Italian woman in her mid to late fifties holding a glass of water in one hand and a jug with ice cubes and a slice of lemon in the other.

'Would you like a drink before you move on?' she asked, passing the frosted glass through the bars of the gate.

'Thank you.' Rachel took the water and drank thirstily. 'I have the most appalling headache.'

'It is the heat,' the woman said refilling the glass Rachel had passed back. 'August is always like this. You are probably dehydrated.'

Rachel drank another glass and another before she gave

the woman a grateful smile as she handed back the glass. '*Grazie.* That literally saved my life.'

'Where are you staying?' the woman asked. 'In Positano or somewhere else?'

Rachel dragged herself to her feet, using the bars of the gate as leverage. 'I haven't got a place to stay,' she said. 'I've got no money to pay for anywhere. And now my luggage has gone missing.'

'You can't stay here,' the woman said. 'Signor Vallini insists on no—'

'I just want five minutes with him,' Rachel said, brushing her damp hair off her face with a weary hand. 'Please? Can you organise that for me? I promise I won't keep him long. Just five minutes of his time is all I'm asking of him.'

The woman set her mouth. 'I could lose my job over this.'

'*Please?*' Rachel couldn't keep the pleading note out of her voice.

The Italian woman let out a long-winded breath as she put the jug and glass down on the flagstones. 'Five minutes but that is all,' she said as she unlocked the gate.

Rachel picked up her handbag and stepped through before the woman changed her mind. The gate was closed and locked behind her with a resounding click that was strangely eerie in the hot still summer air.

The gardens on either side of the entrance to the villa were magnificent. Roses of every colour imaginable bloomed in abundance from behind neatly trimmed ankle-high hedges, their heady sweet fragrance intensified by the sun. There was a huge fountain in the middle of the driveway, the cascading water as Rachel walked past throwing off a fine mist that was deliciously cool and refreshing. She wished she could just stand there and let the soothing spray ease all the tension out of her muscles.

The housekeeper set aside the jug and glass as she opened the front door of the villa. The cooler air of indoors was like a fan as soon as Rachel stepped in. The floor of the foyer was highly polished marble, as was the grand staircase that swept upwards in a two-sided arc that met on the massive landing above. Crystal chandeliers hung above her in glittering elegance, and priceless works of art hung from the walls, the stately windows in between allowing the sunlight to come in via golden shafts that gilded everything it touched.

The villa was breathtaking and so far from the background Alessandro had come from. How had he done it? How had a man who had once been a runaway street kid from the outer suburbs of Melbourne achieved so much in so little time? After working in a variety of jobs after leaving school, at around twenty-four he had started his own one-person landscaping-gardening business while studying part time for a business degree. He had later sold his business as a franchise offering landscaping and gardening services for the top end of the market. Now at thirty-three he owned and operated a business analysis and management empire that had gone global. Had it been her rejection that had fuelled his determination to succeed or had he always been destined to achieve?

'If you will wait here while I speak to Signor Vallini,' the woman said, indicating an antique chair next to a table in the foyer.

Rachel ignored the chair in order to look around. The villa was better than any of the five-star hotels she had ever stayed in and she had stayed in plenty over the years. She had thought her family mansion had been magnificent and certainly compared to many it had been. But this was on another level entirely. This place felt like a palace with its priceless art works and sophisticated decor. She went to a French table with an intricate gold inlay on the top where a vase of roses sat. She touched one of the fragrant blood-red petals and it fell to the table's surface in a velvet silence.

Footsteps sounded behind her and the Italian woman appeared. 'He has agreed to give you five minutes,' she said.

Rachel let out the breath she had been holding and followed the woman up the marble staircase. It was only as she passed a mirror on the second landing that she wished she had asked for a moment or two to freshen up. Her hair was sticky about her too-pink face and the end of her nose looked as if it had caught the sun. Her sleeveless top had damp patches in between her breasts and her shoulder blades, and the crisp white linen trousers she had put on this morning now looked as if they had been worn for a week on an archaeological dig. She didn't look anything like a fashion designer. She looked like a sunburnt, down-on-her-luck vagrant.

The housekeeper knocked on a door on the second level, and, stepping to one side, opened the door for Rachel to go through.

The door closed behind her as Rachel stepped into the room. It was a library—study with three walls of bookshelves and a huge desk set in front of long, heavily curtained windows. Compared to the brightness of the rest of the villa this room seemed dark and brooding, not unlike the man who sat behind the leather-top desk.

Rachel met his eyes across the distance of the room and her heart gave a little involuntary stumble. His eyes were as blue and as deep and as unfathomable as the ocean she had walked past this morning—a startling, incongruous blue given his olive-skinned Italian colouring and jet-black hair.

The silence was like a wall of thick glass dividing the room in two. All Rachel could hear was the sound of her thudding heartbeats. The noiseless air contained a hint of something faintly disturbing. It made her heart beat all the faster and her breathing stalled as if all the air had been sucked out of her lungs.

He had an interesting face. Not handsome in a classical sense but certainly arresting. The Roman nose gave him an aristocratic air, so too did his sharply honed uncompromising jaw.

His mouth was unsmiling.

An errant thought slipped into her head as she wondered when he had last smiled and who had been the recipient of it. A lover perhaps? She had done a little research and found out he had ended a relationship with a cosmetic model a couple of months ago. But there was nothing unusual about that. The same research had turned up that none of his relationships ever lasted more than a month or two. There was nothing else she could find out about his private life other than he was now one of Italy's richest and most eligible men.

'It was very good of you to agree to see me,' she said with forced politeness.

He leaned back in his chair and quietly assessed her with his gaze. It annoyed her that he hadn't even had the decency to rise when she entered the room. Was he doing it deliberately? Of course he was. He wanted to demonstrate his contempt of her and what she had done. But she was not going to be treated like trailer trash. She might have lost just about everything else, but she still had her pride.

'Sit.'

One word.

A command.

An order.

An insult.

Rachel remained standing. 'I won't take up too much of your time,' she said, working hard to control the thread of resentment in her voice.

A corner of his mouth went up in undisguised derision. 'No, indeed you will not,' he said. He flicked his gaze to his expensive-looking watch. 'You had better say what you came here to say and say it quickly, for you have just under four minutes left. I have another commitment straight after this and it has a much higher priority.'

Rachel felt a tremor of anger rumble through her. So this was how he wanted to play it, was it? Sitting on his high horse, deigning to meet with her, only to play cat and mouse with her until he was satisfied he had got his revenge. It had to be about revenge. What else could it be? How he must be gloating about how the tables had turned. The once lowly gardener had made good while the little rich girl was now penniless. 'I want to know if you are the one who sabotaged my attempt to raise finance for my fashion label,' she said, eyeballing him.

His dark eyes held hers steadily. 'I have no idea what you are talking about,' he said.

Rachel was incensed. 'Don't play me for a fool. I know you did it. The executive all but gave me your name.'

He continued to look at her as if she were a small out-of-control child in the middle of a temper tantrum. 'You have your wires crossed, Rachel,' he said in an annoyingly calm voice. 'I have not advised anyone in regards to your label.'

Rachel chewed at the inside of her mouth, fighting for patience. 'I came over to Italy specifically to sign a contract for finance for my label. But as soon as I walked into the office I was told they were no longer going to back me because of the advice they had been given by an expert in business analysis. A highly respected expert.'

He gave a semblance of a smile, a fractional movement of his lips that didn't reveal his teeth. 'I appreciate the compliment that you automatically assumed I was the highly regarded expert, but I can assure you I had nothing to do with it.'

Rachel glared at him furiously. 'I am about to lose everything I've worked so hard for. I had everything riding on that backing and I think you damn well knew it. That's why you did what you did. No one will help me now that they've heard your opinion. But that was your plan, wasn't it? To make me so desperate I would come crawling to you for help.'

He looked at her for a long moment, his eyes quietly assessing her flustered features as he idly rolled a gold pen between his index finger and thumb. 'This little meeting you've cleverly orchestrated,' he said, 'it's all been a ruse to get me to agree to give you money, is it not?'

Rachel was almost beyond rage. 'I've orchestrated nothing! And as for you giving me money I wouldn't dream of…' Her words trailed off as her thoughts ran ahead. What if he *were* to give her the money? He was a very rich man. He had contacts and connections all over Europe that could help her like no one else. Her pride would take a beating, of course, which was probably his intention in the first place, but what was a bit of pride when she stood to lose everything if she didn't secure finance in the next twenty-four hours? '*Would* you agree to give me money?' she asked in a voice that hardly sounded like her own.

He continued to look at her with those incredible blue eyes, steady, watchful, unreadable. 'I would have to know more about your business structure before I made that sort of commitment,' he said. 'Perhaps that is why your previous backers pulled out. Maybe they did a little digging into your background. Perhaps they were worried your fiancé might redirect their hard-earned money into his underworld drug-dealing operation.'

Rachel felt the slap of his statement. The shame of her past rose in her cheeks like a stain that nothing would wash away. She wondered if there would ever come a time when she could put it behind her: her mistakes, her blindness, her stupidity, her stubbornness. 'I am no longer involved with Craig Hughson and I haven't been for over three years.'

Alessandro kept rolling the pen between his finger and thumb. 'So what about your father?' he asked. 'Surely he could spare some of the McCulloch millions to help his daughter?'

Rachel bit her lip, annoyed at herself for not being able to stop the betraying gesture in time. 'I haven't asked him.'

The dark brow lifted again and the rolling of the pen ceased. 'Because he wouldn't be able to help you even if you did ask him, *si*?' he said.

She gripped the strap of her handbag a little tighter. 'I suppose you heard he lost everything three years ago,' she said, hating him for reminding her of it. How he must be relishing in how dramatically the tables had turned. Her father had treated Alessandro appallingly in the time he had worked for him. Why Alessandro had stayed as long as he had had always surprised her. Surely there were other jobs he could have taken without the put-downs and cutting criticisms from her father.

'He always was a gambling man,' Alessandro said. 'What a pity he didn't always measure the risks.'

'Yes…' Rachel mumbled in response. She had found her father's fall from grace extremely upsetting. Not because she was close to him, for, even though she was his only child, she had never managed to do anything to win his approval, apart from agreeing to marry Craig Hughson. But calling off the wedding so close to the day made her feel responsible for her father's bankruptcy. All the money Craig had sunk into the business had been immediately withdrawn. The fact that it had been dirty money didn't ease her conscience one iota. The family business had folded within days and her career as a model had come to one of the most ignominious halts in the history of Melbourne's modelling world when her name and reputation had been sullied in the very public fallout.

The leather of Alessandro's chair squeaked as he shifted his position. 'How much are you after?' he asked.

Rachel's heart gave a little stumble of surprise. 'Y-you'll do it?'

His eyes remained steady on hers. 'For a price.'

She tried to read his inscrutable look. 'Interest, do you mean?'

'Not interest, no.'

She frowned. 'I'm not sure I'm following you,' she said. 'It's financial support I'm after at this point to carry me through to a successful launch in Europe. It will have to be drawn up legally, of course. I'm prepared to pay interest but not if it's unreasonable. I can't stretch myself too far. I have other commitments and—'

'I am not talking about a loan,' he said. 'Consider it a gift.'

Rachel's insides gave a flip flop movement. 'A… a gift?'

His sapphire-blue eyes held hers. 'With conditions.'

'I can't possibly accept a gift of money from you,' she said.

'I insist on paying it back as soon as I can. It might take a while depending on how successful the launch is but—'

'You misunderstand me, Rachel,' he said. 'I am not going to back your label.'

She looked at him in confusion. 'But I thought you said you were going to give me a gift of money?'

'I am.'

Rachel's heart began to beat overtime. 'But I don't understand why you would want to do that,' she said. 'The last time we spoke...' She cleared her throat, not really wanting to recall that dreadful scene on the night of her twenty-first birthday party.

'Aren't you going to ask me what the conditions are?' he asked.

Rachel chewed at her lip. 'If you want me to apologise for how things turned out...um...between us, then I'm sorry,' she said. 'I wanted to tell you about Craig and the expectation that one day we would marry. I *should* have told you. But as soon as you and I started dating I just couldn't seem to do it. I didn't want anything to spoil what we had...'

He remained silent, his face now set in stone.

She took a breath and continued, 'I've had to work so hard to get this far, to be taken seriously after my modelling fiasco. I have people depending on me to make this work. I have staff with mortgages to pay and children to educate and feed. This isn't just about me wanting to prove I can do it. It's not just my money that will be lost if this falls over. My business partner has put everything she has into the company as well. I can't let her down. She's been a good friend to me.'

Alessandro slowly drummed his fingers on the desk as he sat watching her shift from foot to foot. He had waited a long time to hear her apologise for choosing another man's money over his love. But was she apologising out of desperation or real regret?

He studied her features, drinking them in even though he had not for a moment forgotten how she looked. Her grey-green eyes were indelibly imprinted in his brain, so too was her shoulder-length glossy brown hair, the way it caught the sunlight at certain angles bringing out its natural highlights. She had aristocratic cheekbones, and a retroussé nose that gave her heart-shaped face an innocent, childlike air that was at odds with her true personality. She was all innocence on the outside but on the inside she had turned out to be a hard, conniving, conscienceless little opportunist just like every other gold-digger he had known.

Her mouth was something else he had never quite forgotten, but, instead of it being imprinted on his brain, it was for ever imprinted on his lips. He could still feel that pillowy softness beneath his mouth, the way she had opened to him like an exotic flower to the sun. He could still taste the sensual heat of her, the heady temptation she had dangled before him until she had got tired of playing with the hired help and moved on to more affluent pastures.

'I will give you ten thousand euros,' he said into the loaded silence.

'But I need much more than that,' she said, biting at her lower lip.

'Ten thousand and that is all,' he said.

Her grey-green eyes narrowed slightly. 'But why would you do that? If you don't want to back my label then why give me anything at all?'

He gave her a sardonic half-smile. 'Because it will be worth it if you accept my conditions.'

Her eyes flared a little more and the column of her slim

elegant throat slid up and down as she swallowed. 'Wh-what are the conditions?' she asked in a hoarse-sounding voice.

Alessandro held her trapped-in-the-headlights gaze for a pulsing moment.

How ironic she thought he was after revenge when that was the very last thing on his mind right now. 'You can have the money in your bank account within the next half-hour,' he said in a cool and controlled tone, 'but only if you agree to walk out of here and never come back.'

CHAPTER TWO

HER mouth opened and closed and her throat rose and fell again. Her face paled and then flooded with colour. She glared at him, her eyes like flashes of green-tinged lightning, her slim body tight with tension, every muscle contracted in fury. 'You're paying me to…to *leave*?' she asked.

Alessandro leaned back in his chair again. 'Take it or leave it, Rachel. You have one minute to decide before I take the offer off the table. And I won't be making another.'

Her hands clenched in fists by her sides, the action dislodging the precarious sling of her handbag. She shoved it back over her shoulder but the hand that pushed it back was visibly shaking. 'That's outrageous!' she said.

'That's business,' he returned.

'Business?' Her soft lip curled. 'What sort of businessman are you that you have to pay someone to go away?'

'You are not welcome here, Rachel,' he said. 'You want money and appear to be very determined not to leave until you get it. This is a compromise of sorts. For each minute you overstay your welcome the figure will go down.'

She looked at him in bewilderment. Gone was her cocky I'm-a-rich-girl-better-than-you haughtiness, in its place was a shocked, out-of-her-depth ingénue. 'So, let me get this straight…' She ran the tip of her tongue out over her lips before she continued. 'You want me to walk out of here with ten thousand euros of yours, as long as I promise never to return?'

Alessandro gave a single nod.

'But I don't understand,' she went on. 'Why would you want to give me that amount of money for…for essentially nothing?'

'I am a rich man,' Alessandro said, borrowing a bit of her father's philosophy. 'I can do anything I want.'

She pressed her lips together, obviously wondering if she could trust him or not. If he hadn't been feeling so cornered it would have amused him to watch her. She was oscillating, clearly tempted to take things on face value. It wasn't a lot of money by her standards but it was still money. But if things were as precarious as she made out it would at least get her a bed and meals for the rest of her time in Italy. Would she take it and go, or would she try and weasel some more out of him?

He glanced at his watch. 'The figure is now nine thousand euros, Rachel,' he said. 'What is your decision?'

Her eyes moved away from his, the colour on her cheeks still high. 'You have to understand if this was just about me I would have walked out of here five minutes ago,' she said. 'In fact I wouldn't have come here in the first place if it hadn't been for what you did to sabotage—'

'You are robbing yourself of another thousand.'

She met his gaze again, her tongue sweeping over the surface of her lips again. 'Can I have a little more time to think about this?' she asked.

'No.'

'But that's crazy!' she said. 'How do I know I can trust you? You might give me the money and then change the rules.'

'I will not change the rules,' he said. 'I simply want you to take the money and leave.'

Her mouth flattened in anger. 'This is payback, isn't it? You want to make me pay for how I chose Craig instead of you.'

Alessandro kept his expression bland, uninterested, totally unmoved. 'If you don't want the money I am sure I can find someone else who does.'

'But I need much more than that amount,' she said. 'I need to get my—'

'That is all I am prepared to give you,' he said. 'Now please make up your mind before the amount left is not worth taking.'

She shifted her weight agitatedly, her mouth opening and snapping closed as if she was not quite ready to allow the words out. 'I will accept your offer,' she finally said.

'Good,' Alessandro said. 'Give me your account details and I will transfer the funds as soon as I see you walk out of that gate.'

She wrote them on a piece of paper and passed them across. 'So that's it?' she asked. 'You don't even want to offer me a drink or a meal or anything?'

'No, you can get that at your hotel.'

'I haven't got a hotel,' she said, 'or at least not yet.'

'I am sure you will find one. Positano is full of them suitable for most price brackets.'

'But I haven't got any luggage. It's been misplaced. I don't know when it's going to turn up, if ever.'

'Not my problem,' he said.

'You heartless bastard,' she railed at him. 'Don't you care about anyone but yourself?'

He elevated one of his dark brows. 'I have taken a leaf out

of your book, Rachel,' he said. 'I no longer do anything to please anyone but myself.'

'Do you have to pay your lovers to arrive as well as leave?' she asked with a biting look. 'You have a quick turnover of women in your life, or so I have heard.'

'So you have been reading about me in the press, have you, Rachel?' he asked, allowing himself a small smile of satisfaction.

'The Australian press don't have access to too many details of your life,' she said, 'but now and again one of the UK magazines I occasionally buy mentions you and your latest girlfriend on the society pages.'

'Does it seem ironic to you that the man you turned down all those years ago is now richer and more powerful than both your father and your ex-fiancé combined?' Alessandro asked.

'How did you do it?' she asked, but then bit down on her lip as if she had regretted the words as soon as she had said them.

'I was prepared for success and jumped at it when the first opportunity presented itself,' he said. 'Leaving Australia and coming over here opened up new avenues for me that would not have occurred otherwise.'

'It's a shame you don't have any family to be proud of you,' she said.

Alessandro clenched his jaw at her little jibe. He was used to her throwing her blue-blood lines in his face in the past. She was the rich girl with the pedigree; he was the abandoned mongrel who trawled the streets for the scraps thrown to him. He hated her for tricking him into thinking he'd had a chance with her. She had lured him into her sweet honey trap before flicking him away like an annoying insect. He was not going to make that mistake again, not with her or any woman. 'Yes, but I have many friends who more than make up for the lack of close family,' he said. 'Now if you will excuse me I have work to do.'

'Aren't you going to accompany me to the door of your fortress to make sure I don't pinch the silver on the way out?' she asked.

'I will leave Lucia to escort you off the property,' Alessandro said. 'I have better things to do with my time.'

'She seems very nice,' Rachel said, deliberately stalling. 'Your housekeeper, I mean.'

'Lucia is a kind soul,' he said. 'She has worked for me ever since I came to Italy. She is like a mother to me.'

Rachel thought of her own mother, an increasingly vague, amorphous image that drifted in and out of her consciousness from time to time. She had died when Rachel was three and a half but she still missed her. There was a mother-shaped hole inside her that nothing and no one had filled since in spite of her father's many and varied partners over the years. She wondered if Alessandro, without either of his parents in his life, felt the same. He had never said. He had never talked of his childhood. All she knew from what little she had heard from others was he had spent a lot of time in foster homes or on the streets while growing up. Maybe his parents were dead. Maybe they were alive. Maybe he didn't want to know.

Alessandro pressed an intercom button on his desk and summoned Lucia. 'Miss McCulloch is ready to leave.'

'Sì, Signor,' Lucia answered. 'I will come now.'

Rachel didn't like being dismissed. It irritated the hell out of her that he just sat there issuing orders. She wanted more time with him so she could irritate him right back. Her anger towards him bubbled up inside her. She wanted to grab him by the front of his immaculate shirt and tell him exactly what she thought of him. 'You're really getting a kick out of this, aren't you?' she said.

'Careful, Rachel,' he said, eyeballing her darkly. 'Don't go biting the hand that is about to pay for your next meal.'

Lucia arrived at that moment. 'Signorina? I will see you to the gate,' she said, holding the study door open.

'Thank you,' Rachel said, but not before flinging one last cutting glare to Alessandro. 'Goodbye, Alessandro. I hope I never have to see you again.'

He didn't answer, which irritated her even more.

Alessandro watched as his housekeeper accompanied Rachel to the front entrance of the villa. He clenched and unclenched his hands on the side of his chair in rising tension. He turned away from the window and stared at his computer screen sightlessly. A couple of months ago he would have paid her to stay. He would have paid her to occupy his bed. He would have enjoyed showing her all she had missed out on in choosing Craig Hughson over him. And then he would have cast her adrift, coldly, callously, just as she had done to him.

But everything was different now.

He couldn't afford to let her know what had happened to him. So far only his housekeeper and doctor and physical therapist knew. People in business were unpredictable, fickle at the whisper of a personal problem. One word in the press that he had suffered a health setback such as this could jeopardise his negotiations for the biggest coup of his career. A massively wealthy sheikh from Dubai was considering using Alessandro's business analysis services. It was the sort of contact that would bring in even more wealthy clients, those with the sort of wealth that outshone even his current ones. He didn't want anything to compromise the already tricky negotiations. The doctor had told him he needed another month of rehabilitation. One more month of privacy and then he could get on with his life.

The intercom sounded on his desk and he leaned forward to answer. 'Yes, Lucia?'

'I had to bring Miss McCulloch back into the villa,' Lucia said.

'Why?' he barked the word at her.

'She's not well. I think she has a touch of heatstroke.'

Alessandro drummed his fingers on the desk until his fingertips went numb. His conscience jabbed at him again. He could hardly send her away ill. He could probably get away with a couple of days and nights with her in the villa without revealing the extent of his condition. Lucia would be discreet. It might even be amusing to see Rachel leave at the end of her brief stay with no idea of what he was hiding from her and the world at large. 'All right,' he said to his housekeeper. 'Put her in one of the guest suites well away from mine. Does she need to see a doctor?'

'I don't think so,' Lucia said. 'She just needs to get some fluids on board and rest for a day or two. She is still a little jet-lagged.'

'You're too soft, Lucia,' Alessandro said gruffly.

'Maybe, but she seems a nice young woman,' Lucia said.

'You don't know her like I do,' he said. 'For all you know this could be an act.'

'It's not an act,' Lucia said. 'She was sick a few minutes ago. I had to half carry her back to the villa. I thought she was going to pass out.'

Alessandro frowned. 'Are you sure she doesn't need a doctor?'

'I will call one if she doesn't improve after a rest,' Lucia said. 'I think she'll be a lot better by tomorrow.'

Alessandro sat back in his chair once the conversation ended. One or two days was all he was prepared to allow Rachel to stay. It was risky, but then wasn't everything in life that was enjoyable? A slow smile tugged at his mouth as he thought of entertaining her. It would be quite diverting to see her grovel for more money. He assumed that was what she would do. She hadn't got what she wanted from him and would surely have another go to achieve her goal. He wondered how far she would take things. What sort of artifice would she employ this time to get him to lower his guard? He would play along with it, reeling her in just as she had done him, and then he would pull the rug from under her feet.

That would be the most entertaining part of it all.

Rachel woke from a deep and refreshing sleep. She looked at the clock by the bed and was shocked to see she had slept the clock around. Her headache had thankfully gone and the grumbling nausea had passed. Her temperature was normal and after a shower she felt almost human again, even though she had no choice but to put the same clothes back on, although the housekeeper had very kindly laundered and pressed them for her. Rachel had yet to hear from the bus company about the whereabouts of her luggage. There were no messages on her phone and no missed calls.

Her mobile rang from beside the bed and she reached across to answer it. 'Hello?'

'So how did it go?' Caitlyn asked. 'I've been waiting for hours and hours for you to tell me. Did you get the backing?'

'No, not exactly,' Rachel said and quickly filled in her friend and business partner on what had occurred.

'Gosh, that's disappointing,' Caitlyn said. 'Do you think you can have another talk to him about it?'

'I'll try but I don't think it's going to work,' Rachel said. 'He's only allowing me to stay here now because I was ill yesterday. And that was only after the housekeeper put the hard word on him.'

'He sounds very bitter.'

'He is,' Rachel said. 'He looked at me with such loathing I found it unnerving.'

'Well, you did turn down his marriage proposal in the past,' Caitlyn said. 'Some men find rejection really hard to take.'

'But I wasn't sure if I loved him enough to marry him,' Rachel said in her defence.

'You didn't love Craig either,' Caitlyn reminded her.

'I know,' Rachel said, feeling a cringe of shame at how she had handled things. In an effort to please her unpleasable father she had chosen money over a man's love. Alessandro had told her he loved her. Even her father had never said those three little words. Craig had never said them either.

Rachel hated thinking of the two years of hell she had lived through being engaged to Craig Hughson. Thank God she hadn't married him. She had come close but had found out just in time about his double life. How could she have been so naive to have allowed him to control her the way he had? It had taken the last couple of years to move on but, even so, now and again something would appear in the press about his underworld connections and it would bring it all back to her. This latest red flag on her account made her worry that she might never be able to put it behind her.

This much-anticipated trip to Italy was the first time she had felt a glimmer of hope that her luck was going to change, that she would find her feet again, be the success she had always dreamed she could be, not because of her looks, not because of her family background, but because of her own hard work. The sudden withdrawal of financial backing had knocked her sideways. But that had surely been Alessandro's plan. He had deviously engineered things so that he could maximise her humiliation.

She hated him for it.

There was a knock on the door and the housekeeper, Lucia, announced that refreshments would be served out by the pool if she felt up to joining Alessandro. Feeling hopelessly unprepared, Rachel made her way down to the pool area. She had no bathing costume. Her bikini was in the luggage somewhere between here and Milan. Not that Alessandro had shown much interest in her as a woman, she thought. She could probably turn up naked and he wouldn't blink. She had tried to gauge his expression during their brief meeting to see if he gave off any signals of physical interest, but to her chagrin he had not. She was annoyed with herself for feeling piqued. She was not vain; well, certainly not as vain as she had been in her youth. Craig's constant put-downs had more or less destroyed her self-esteem, and in the years since she had worked hard to build up her confidence again. But she wouldn't be female if she didn't appreciate the occasional compliment, either verbal or non-verbal. But while Alessandro hadn't said or shown any interest, there had been that faintly disturbing undercurrent in the room. She still felt it now, the dusting of goose bumps on her skin when she thought of his dark blue unwavering gaze holding hers...

The terrace where the pool was situated was drenched in warm afternoon sunlight with a light breeze coming in from the ocean so far down below. Rachel felt her heart give a little kick when she saw Alessandro was in the pool, swimming in long easy strokes, his arms slicing through the water effortlessly, his long tanned legs barely needing to kick for the powerful strength in his upper body. She couldn't stop looking at him, the way the muscles of his back and shoulders bunched beneath his tanned skin with each movement he made. The way the water sluiced off his hard male flesh in shiny droplets that splashed like diamonds as they fell back into the pool. He didn't tumble turn at the end, but stopped and looked up and met her eyes with his water-spiked dark, thickly lashed blue ones.

'Do you have swimwear with you?' he asked, glancing at her white linen trousers and top.

'No, I didn't think I would be staying any longer than a few minutes,' she said, feeling her colour rise in her cheeks. 'And I'm still waiting to hear from the bus company about my luggage.'

'Lucia can find something for you,' he said. 'I am sure there are bikinis somewhere upstairs from previous guests.'

Rachel put up her chin. 'I am not wearing one of your ex-lovers' cast-offs.'

His eyes gleamed. 'Then you will have to swim naked, won't you?'

Rachel felt the searing heat of his gaze as it ran over her from head to toe. She felt as if every article of clothing she wore were suddenly transparent. Her skin burned and tingled, her breasts tightened and peaked against her bra, and her inner thighs flickered with a sensation she flatly refused to identify as desire. She hated him more every minute she spent in his company. He was an annoying reminder of all the mistakes she had made in the past. She didn't like the way those critical dark blue eyes made her feel so exposed. She felt he could see right through her poise and sophisticated veneer to the insecure woman she still felt on the inside. He had always made her feel that way. She had never been able to hide behind her social standing with him. He threatened her in a way she could not handle. He still had that powerful effect on her and she didn't have a clue how to manage it or counteract it. 'I am perfectly fine sitting out here,' she said coldly.

'Suit yourself,' he said, brushing his wet hair back off his face with one of his hands.

Rachel rolled her lips together, wishing she could tear her gaze away from the broad expanse of his chest, but her eyes were like two iron filings being lured by a powerful magnet. His pectoral muscles were so well defined. He must be lifting bulldozers in the gym, she thought. Unlike a lot of men of his generation he had resisted removing the masculine sprinkling of hair that went from a T shape across his chest to a narrow trail that disappeared beneath the black bathers he was wearing. She was glad the edge of the pool prevented her from looking any further. She had more than once felt the hard ridge of his maleness against her lower body when he had kissed her in the past. Her response to him back then had totally shocked her. It had shamed her that she had been so wanton with him, that in his arms she had turned into a ravenous tigress desperate for his kisses and his searing touch.

He was not the type of man her father had wanted her to associate with. He was beneath her in every way imaginable, he was untouchable, he was forbidden fruit. But still she had been drawn to him time and time again, unable to stop herself from stealing clandestine moments with him. Her behaviour had been unpardonable. She had led Alessandro on shamelessly when all the time she had never had any intention of going against her father's wishes.

Rachel became aware of Alessandro's gaze on hers and wondered if he was remembering those few stolen passionate kisses and that final showdown the night of her twenty-first birthday party when her engagement to Craig had been formally announced. It still made her heart jerk painfully when she recalled the look in Alessandro's eyes that night. She had never seen such loathing, such contempt and anger. It had been red-hot. It had scorched her to the backbone. No wonder he still wanted to punish her.

She swallowed the tense knot in her throat, hating that she was hot and sticky and perspiring while he looked so cool and composed. It was ironic that he was the one in deep water, but, although she was standing on the rock-steady sun-baked flagstones, she felt as if she were in over her head.

'Lucia has left drinks on the table over there in the shade,' Alessandro said. 'Would you mind bringing me a cold beer?'

Rachel glanced at the tray of drinks and then pursed her lips when she faced him again. 'Why don't you get it yourself?' she said.

'I am enjoying the water too much,' he said.

She folded her arms in a recalcitrant manner. 'I am not your slave.'

He gave her a slow smile that sent another shock wave between her thighs. It unsettled her so much she turned on her heel and stomped over to the drinks and poured herself an ice-cold wine. She sat down on the terrace furniture, crossing one leg over the other as she sipped from her glass. She had almost finished the wine and he still hadn't moved from the side of the pool.

She knew he was watching her. She felt the weight of his

gaze. She had always been aware of him watching her in the past. She had developed a sixth sense where he was concerned. She poured herself another wine and began sipping it, slower this time, aware that she was probably still a little low on fluids given how warm it was. The last thing she wanted to do was lose her head while in the presence of Alessandro Vallini.

God, she was *so* hot. Why hadn't she packed a bikini in her handbag? It would have taken no space. Why hadn't she thought? Luggage went missing all the time. It was one of the drags of travelling. She should have been more prepared. She pushed some sticky strands of hair off her face and took another cautious sip of her wine.

'Have you got sunscreen on?' Alessandro said.

'Have you?' she threw back.

'I always use protection.'

Rachel felt that disturbing quiver again deep and low in her belly and to distract herself, jumped up and snatched a cold lager off the tray and took it to him. 'Do you want a glass with that?'

'No, this is fine. Thank you.'

She watched as he tipped his head back and drank from the bottle, the column of his long strong throat making her wonder what his skin would taste like if she were to trail her tongue along the dark stubble along his jaw…

She shied away from her traitorous thoughts like a cat springing away from a snapping dog. She went back to the chair in the shade and picked up her wine, holding it with both of her hands to control their sudden trembling. She had definitely been too long in the sun or something. She was acting so out of character. She wasn't the type to be affected by a hot body and a slow sensual curve of a smile. Not any more.

She was sensible and sorted out now. Life had taught her to get her priorities in order. No more infatuations, no more silly little dreams of being loved unconditionally. Everyone was out for what they could get and she was no different. She wished she could make him change his mind about backing her, however. If only she had more time with him to convince him of the potential of her label. If she could just get him to sit down with her and look at her spring and summer collection surely he would see how serious she was about this? How could she get him to change his mind?

Alessandro finished his beer and set the bottle well back from the edge of the pool. 'Are you sure you won't join me?' he asked.

'No, thank you.'

'You could swim in your bra and knickers,' he said. He waited a beat and added with another glint in his eyes, 'You *are* wearing a bra and knickers, aren't you?'

Rachel's face felt like a furnace. How she hated him for taunting her like this. He was reminding her of the times when he had been at her father's estate in the early years when she had deliberately paraded her scantily clad body before him. She had thought it amusing back then. It had made her feel so powerful. But now he was the one with all the power.

'Of course I am wearing underwear,' she said primly.

'I am sure it is far more modest than some of the bikinis I have seen in this pool,' he said.

Rachel could just imagine the minuscule scraps of fabric his lovers would prance around in. Not that she could talk. She had worn plenty of racy little numbers herself in the past. And he had seen her in them too. She had made sure of it. These days she went for a more classic look. 'I might come down later after you've gone,' she said.

'I'm not planning on leaving any time soon,' he said. 'I swim for an hour each day, sometimes twice a day.'

Hence the strong pecs, Rachel thought. 'That seems rather excessive,' she said. 'Are you training for something? The next Olympics maybe?' She didn't care that she sounded sarcastic. She didn't see why she should pull any punches with him. He had insulted her from the moment she had stepped into his presence. It wasn't helping her cause, she knew, but it sure felt good to give as good as she got from him.

His expression became shuttered, closed off, shadowed. 'I like the exercise,' he said. 'It's good for the mind as well as the body.'

He resumed swimming, length after length, the same rhythmic action having an almost hypnotic effect on her as she watched from the shade.

She sat for a bit longer finishing her wine, and in spite of the overhanging branches of the tree beside the table and chairs the heat became a torment. Perhaps it was the wine, perhaps it was the heat, or perhaps it was the streak of wilfulness in her personality that refused to let Alessandro think he could win any tussles with her.

She stood up and slipped out of her sandals and linen trousers and top, leaving them folded over the back of the chair she had just vacated. The bra and knickers ensemble she was wearing was thankfully a decent set Caitlyn had bought her for her last birthday. It was white with tiny pink rosebuds sewn in between the cups of the bra and on the front of the knickers. It covered her far more than some of the bikinis she had worn in the past, but even so as she walked towards the pool she felt as naked as the day she had been born.

Alessandro was at the other end of the pool when she slipped into the water but he turned to look at her as if some internal radar had signalled to him she had joined him. 'Changed your mind?' he said.

'I was practically melting out there,' she said, disguising a sigh of pure bliss as the cool water embraced her.

'You should be used to the heat coming from Melbourne.'

'It's winter there now and it's been a cold one,' she said.

He leaned against the end of the pool in an indolent pose. 'Come over here,' he said. 'It's deeper.'

'I'm fine here,' Rachel said. 'I like to be able to touch the bottom.'

'You can still swim, can't you?'

'Of course, but I'm clearly not in quite the same league as you,' she said.

'I've been putting in a little extra practice just lately,' he said in a tone touched with wryness as he effortlessly hauled himself out of the pool to sit on the edge, his legs still dangling in the water.

Rachel's eyes went to his flat abdomen seemingly of their own volition. There was not a spare gram of flesh on him. Every abdominal muscle was clearly defined as if drawn by an anatomy artist. Her fingers itched to explore those hard ridges, to feel the texture of his skin, to tiptoe through the hair that marked him as a healthy potent male. Her heart began to beat heavily and she hadn't even swum a stroke. Her breathing too was uneven, stopping and starting in her chest as if her lungs were being squeezed on and off by a large hand.

'Are you going to do a length or two?' Alessandro asked.

'Are you going to criticise me if I don't do it like a professional athlete?' she tossed back archly.

He gave a slow, lopsided smile. 'You need to learn to take constructive criticism, Rachel,' he said. 'How else can one learn to improve oneself if one is not open to feedback?'

Rather than answer him she slipped into the water and began swimming. She had never been more conscious of her body, and yet she had strutted on catwalks in several major cities before her career had been blown apart by her ex-fiancé's double life in dealing drugs being exposed.

She got to the other end of the pool and had to draw breath. Obviously her fitness was something she needed to work on.

'You need to stop fighting the water,' Alessandro said from where he was sitting on the poolside. 'You're making it harder for yourself. You're expending twice as much energy as you need to.'

She pushed the hair back off her face. 'Yes, well, it's not easy when I can't see where the heck I am going.'

'You need to tie your hair back or wear a swimming cap, goggles too, if you don't like the water in your eyes.'

'If I had known I was booking in for boot camp I would have packed accordingly,' she said tartly.

His mouth was tilted in that half-smile again. 'Try another lap without thrashing the water,' he said. 'Let the water support you as you move through it.'

Rachel went back and it did seem a little easier this time. She wasn't quite so breathless, although that soon changed when she saw the way Alessandro glanced at her breasts. Heat flowed through her at the intimate contact. It felt as if he had touched her, cupping her with those broad strong hands of his. Her skin tingled in response, her nipples peaking as if he had just brushed the pads of his thumbs over them. There was no way of hiding her reaction to him. Could he tell? Did he know what he was doing to her? Was he remembering how he had once brushed his hot mouth against her tightly budded nipple in a stolen moment in the summer house?

His eyes came back to hers and held firm. 'How about trying some breaststroke?' he suggested.

Rachel gave him a look. 'I just bet you're an expert at that.'

His eyes glinted. 'You could say I'm very experienced.'

Her belly flickered and fluttered at his double entendre. She slipped back into the water and did her version of the stroke, which she had always felt was more of a combination of a dog trying not to drown and a frog with a wonky leg. That Alessandro thought so too was more than apparent when she saw the grimace on his face when she stopped at his end. 'Needs some work?' she asked.

'What a pity you aren't staying longer than forty-eight hours,' he said. 'I could have given you some free tuition.'

'I could always stay a little longer,' she said, blinking the droplets of water out of her eyes. 'My return ticket isn't until the first of September.'

He held her look for a pulsing moment. 'Two days, Rachel. That's all. I want you out of here by tomorrow morning.'

Rachel felt her resentment building all over again. He was practically throwing her out on the street. What had happened to good old-fashioned hospitality? Did he really hate her that much? 'But what if my luggage doesn't turn up by then?' she asked.

'You'll have to buy some clothes with the money I gave you.'

'But practically all the money you gave me is going to be used up to pay off debts back home,' she said.

'Then you will have to find a job to tide you over.'

Lucia came out at that point and Alessandro frowned when he saw the harried look on her face.

'Lucia? Is something wrong?' he asked in Italian.

'*Sì, Signor,*' Lucia said, wringing her hands agitatedly. 'I am afraid I have a family emergency to attend to. My daughter-in-law has been admitted to hospital. There is a problem with her pregnancy. My son needs me to babysit my grandsons. I am so sorry. I must go. I will hopefully only be away for a night, two at the most. I called Carlotta to fill in for me but she is visiting her mother in Sicily.'

Rachel had no real idea of what was being said since they spoke in such rapid Italian but it was clear Alessandro was not happy about something. A heavy frown pulled at his brows and his jaw tightened like a clamp.

Lucia glanced at Rachel before turning back to her employer, this time speaking in English. 'What about Miss McCulloch?'

'No. Non è assolutemente,' he said firmly.

'But she is already here with nowhere else to go until her luggage arrives,' Lucia continued. 'She could fill in until I get back or until we find a replacement.'

'Is there something I can do to help?' Rachel offered.

Alessandro frowned heavily. 'No. I do not need your help.'

Lucia wrung her hands some more. *'Signor*, please, I beg you. I must leave as soon as I possibly can. My son is waiting for me so he can be with his wife. I need to pack a few things before I go.'

'All right,' Alessandro said. 'Do what you have to do. I will see what can be arranged.'

Lucia bustled off, her flat sensible shoes almost flying across the flagstones in her haste.

'I take it there's been some sort of an emergency,' Rachel said.

'Yes,' Alessandro said. 'It seems I am without a housekeeper for the next day or two unless I can find a replacement.'

'I could always fill in for Lucia,' she said. 'I can cook and I can clean.'

Alessandro looked down at her upturned face. Could he risk it? Could he employ her for the next couple of days and wear the consequences? It would solve one problem even if it threw up some others. He knew the press was already wondering why he was here without a mistress. Since his break-up with Lissette there had been speculation over who would take her place. Who better than the young woman who had turned him down in the past? It would be different this time of course. He would employ her. It would be a business deal. They would both get what they wanted. No emotional involvement, just cold hard cash. He would have to protect himself legally, of course. He would get his legal people to draw up an agreement immediately. One indiscreet word to the press from her and his business deal could be jeopardised. But he was prepared to risk it if it meant he could have Rachel at his beck and call even for a day or two. She had no idea what she was taking on. That was part of the appeal for him. She would leave as soon as she found out, he was sure of it. It would prove to him all over again that she was without compassion, without a care for anyone but herself. And right now he needed reminding of it. Having her here had already awakened urges he had soused with cynicism years ago. Her sassiness and spirited and wilful nature excited him much more than any of the compliant partners he'd had over the years.

'You really want to work for me?' he asked.

She nodded. 'If working for you for a few days will convince you to consider backing my label, then yes, I will do whatever you want me to do.'

Alessandro hooked one brow upwards. 'Anything?'

A flicker of uncertainty came and went in her gaze. 'Anything within reason,' she said.

'Just how far are you prepared to go for the financial backing you require?' he asked.

Her teeth snagged at her full bottom lip. 'Pretty far…'

'I am known to be a hard taskmaster, Rachel,' Alessandro said. 'Do you think you'll be able to satisfy my exacting standards?'

Her cheeks flushed with delicate colour as she valiantly held his gaze. 'I will do my best to give the best service possible,' she said.

'Do you realise that by sharing the villa with me even for a couple of days that people will jump to conclusions about what exactly is the nature of our relationship?' he said.

The colour on her cheeks deepened. 'It's been my experience that people will think what they like no matter what the truth is,' she said.

'As long as you understand you are under my employ as a fill-in housekeeper,' he said. 'Don't go getting any ideas of filling in other areas of my life.'

She gave him a withering look. 'You would have to pay me a king's ransom to become your latest mistress,' she said.

Alessandro felt his lower spine zap with searing heat at her defiant words. His groin burned with the sudden flash fire of longing, a burgeoning heat that threatened to overthrow every bit of his resolve to have nothing to do with her. He had always wanted to tame her shrewish streak and now was a perfect opportunity to do it. 'Dangerous words, Rachel,' he warned silkily. 'Don't go throwing challenges down at me like that. I might just take you up on it.'

CHAPTER THREE

RACHEL glared at him. 'People like you think you can buy anything you want, don't you? But I am not selling myself, and certainly not to you.'

'Sleeping rough not your thing any more, little rich girl?' Alessandro asked with a mocking slant to his mouth.

She ground her teeth. 'I am offering to work as your house-keeper, nothing else.'

'I think it will be quite diverting to have you around waiting on me hand and foot,' he said. 'This is quite a change in circumstances, *sì*? I'll have to find something really menial for you to do. I wonder if you will be able to handle it.'

Rachel hauled herself out of the pool with a strength she had not known she possessed. She flung her wet hair back from her face and glared down at him. There was something about him just sitting there with his long tanned legs dangling in the pool that sent her anger skyrocketing. He was acting so cool and collected, so calm and clinical, so in control—of her. 'You bastard,' she said through lips trembling with rage. 'I bet you planned this right from the start.'

'I haven't planned anything, Rachel,' he said in the same calm even tone. 'I have simply offered you a business proposition. That is all this is: a temporary contract between us. Once Lucia is back you are free to go.'

She put her hands on her hips and continued to glare down at him. 'So you're not even going to consider backing my label?'

'One thing you need to know about me, Rachel, is I don't rush headlong into things without serious consideration,' he said. 'I am not putting my name to something that is not worthy of my time and commitment and hard-earned money.'

'Will you at least look at my designs and my business plan?' she asked.

'I will consider it if you behave yourself.'

'You mean if I sleep with you,' she said with a hardened look.

His eyes slowly moved over her, leaving a smouldering path on her flesh in their wake. 'Is that the way you normally conduct business?' he asked.

'No, of course not!' Rachel said. 'I just assumed you would want to—'

'You should not assume anything when it comes to me,' he said with one of his enigmatic barely there smiles.

Rachel felt emotionally stranded. What did he want from her if not to sleep with her? Their brief affair had not been consummated five years ago. Wouldn't forcing her to sleep with him for money be the perfect revenge? In the past he had always only ever touched her once she had given him encouragement, which was more than she could say for her ex-fiancé who had seemed to think he could do anything he wanted whenever he wanted irrespective of her wishes.

But if Alessandro were to sleep with her he would find her a very poor partner, certainly nothing like the exotic and physically confident women he was used to. It would be so humiliating to have him find out how limited she was sensually. But for all her inadequacies sexually, she still felt an electrifying energy in the air when she was with him, an undercurrent of sensual heat that was visceral. She felt the dancing nerves of her skin when his eyes rested on her. She felt the stirring of her blood, the escalation of her pulse every time he spoke in that rich, deep, well-modulated voice of his. He was having a tumultuous effect on her senses that she could not in any way control. Was he aware of it? Was that his intention in having her here like this? To show her how it felt to be the one spurned? Why hadn't she realised one day there would be a price to pay?

'I will give you the rest of the day to think it over,' Alessandro said. 'I will have an agreement drawn up legally. It will be ready by dinner for you to sign.'

Rachel frowned at him. 'An agreement? What sort of agreement? Why does it have to be so formal?'

'By agreeing to live here with me for even a day or two you will be required to sign a contract that forbids you to speak to the press,' he said.

'You don't trust my word?' she asked.

'You should go and shower,' Alessandro said, ignoring her question. 'You will burn if you stay in the sun any longer.'

'Are you coming in now?' Rachel asked, not really liking the feeling of being summarily dismissed.

'No, I want to swim some more,' he said. 'I'll see you at dinner. I hope you can find your way around the kitchen. Lucia keeps it well stocked. I would like to dine at eight-thirty and I expect you to dine with me.'

'Isn't that a bit unusual?' she asked. 'You don't take any of your meals with Lucia.'

'This is an entirely different situation,' he said. 'You are here as a guest as well as a temporary employee.'

'I'm not really a guest though, am I?' she said. 'You never wanted me here in the first place, or so you said.'

'If I am not the most welcoming host you have only yourself to blame,' he said. 'But now that you are here I am prepared to make the best of it. I suggest you do the same.'

Rachel collected her dress and sandals but decided against dressing and instead took one of the towels that was lying on the sun lounge and used it like a sarong. She glanced back at the pool but Alessandro was still sitting on the edge looking at the water, a frown pulling at his brow. Her heart gave another tiny unexpected squeeze but she quickly shook off the sensation and walked back into the villa and up the staircase to her room.

She wasn't sure why she went to the window but she found her feet taking her there as if they had developed a mind of their own. She looked down to the terrace below but there was no sign of Alessandro in the pool. He was no longer sitting on the edge either. There was no sign of him anywhere.

She moved towards the en suite but when she came out after her shower she could hear in the background the mechanical whirr of some kind of machinery from deep within the villa. A lift perhaps? She assumed it was Lucia leaving to go to her family. Maybe the housekeeper found the four flights of stairs too much given she had to keep the massive villa in order, which she seemed to do with meticulous care, Rachel thought as she looked longingly at the pristine bed.

A short nap before she started on dinner would hopefully prepare her for another verbal fight with Alessandro. She didn't like admitting it but she was almost looking forward to it.

After her rest Rachel changed back into her linen trousers and top. She had no jewellery other than a tiny diamond pendant that had been her mother's. She never went anywhere without it. She had no make-up to put on. Her cosmetics bag was inside her luggage, which had still not been located. She had a tube of lip gloss in her handbag, which made her feel marginally less unsophisticated. She pulled her hair back into an elegant chignon at the back of her head. It was her power hairdo; no stray hairs to make her look like a child that had just come in from playing in the back garden.

She walked down the staircase, her hand sliding down the cool marble as she went. She had to find her way to the kitchen on her own, but then she hadn't been given a tour. Alessandro had been adamant about the two-day limit on her stay, but now with Lucia's family crisis working in her favour she had a window of opportunity to change his mind about backing her. How to get him to change his mind was something that was certainly going to be a challenge. The money he had given her would not last the week given the state of the company's finances. Would she go as far as to beg for his help? Was that what he wanted her to do? He was such an intriguing man: mysterious, aloof and so disturbingly, tantalisingly male. Living with him as his housekeeper for a day or two would test her in ways she had not expected to be tested. She hadn't expected to still feel that strange flutter of nerves every time he looked at her. His gaze was like a physical touch. She felt it following her every move. She felt the stirring of her blood, the heating of her flesh as if his gaze were a brand sealing the invisible connection she felt each time she was in his presence.

She decided she would have to be careful.

Very careful.

The kitchen was a cook's dream and there was no short-age of fresh and store-cupboard ingredients to whip up a gourmet meal. Rachel dived into the task, determined to show Alessandro how capable she was. Long gone were the days of hiring cooks and cleaners to do the work for her. She had learned a lot over the last few years and took pride in being able to cook for a couple or a crowd.

Rachel hadn't heard Alessandro enter the dining room. She came in to put the finishing touches to the table to find him already seated at the head of the table next to the bottle of champagne and white wine she had placed in an ice bucket earlier.

'Dinner won't be long,' she said. 'I just have to check the chicken casserole.'

'I said dinner was to be at eight-thirty,' he said, challenging her with his dark blue eyes.

Rachel felt her back come up. 'My watch says it's only eight-twenty.'

'Then your watch must be wrong,' he returned.

'Are you usually so pedantic about mealtimes or is this just for my benefit?' she asked.

'You are now under my employ, Rachel,' he said. 'I will not tolerate sloppiness or unpunctuality in any form.'

She tried to stare him down but in the end she had to look away. Resentment burned inside her like hot coals as she flounced back to the kitchen to bring in the meal.

He was still sitting at the head of the table when she came in with their starter. She placed it before him and went to stand by her place opposite. It annoyed her again how he just sat there like a king waiting for his subjects to appear before him. He must be doing it on purpose, to make her feel she was not worth the effort of acknowledging her or by rising when she came into the room. The very least he could have done was to stand up and pull out her chair for her. 'I'm surprised you haven't started on your food before I've even sat down,' she said.

'It is the height of rudeness to begin eating one's meal until every guest is seated at the table and has each been served their meal,' Alessandro said.

'It is also rude for a man not to rise when a lady enters the room,' Rachel quickly shot back.

He looked past her as if looking for some other guest to appear. 'I had not noticed any ladies enter the room,' he said with a cool stretch of his lips that kept his teeth concealed. 'Perhaps you will inform me if and when one does.'

Rachel clenched her hands on the back of the chair in case she was tempted to slap him for his insulting slight. 'You're really enjoying this, aren't you?' she said. 'You're getting a sick sense of enjoyment out of this turn of the tables. Your lord-of-the-manor routine is pathetic. No amount of wealth is going to be able to change your background. You can white-wash it all you like with your wealthy surroundings and price-less possessions but underneath it all you are still a rough kid from the suburbs who got lucky.'

'Sit,' he said, his eyes locked on hers, fire meeting ice.

She gripped the chair even harder, defiance pushing her chin forward. 'I will sit when you stand.'

'You will be waiting a long time, Rachel,' he said. 'Now sit before I lose my temper.'

The air began to crackle as if charged with thousands of volts of electricity as his dark sapphire eyes held hers in a powerful lockdown.

A feather of unease danced up Rachel's spine. There was no visible sign of anger on his face, but she felt it all the same. It was invisible but very, very real. It moved around her, closing in on her like invisible coils that were tightening her chest with every beat of her heart.

The silence throbbed and throbbed but then he broke it by saying, 'I have the papers here for you to sign.' He passed them to her.

Rachel hesitated, but then she took them with an unsteady hand. It annoyed her how the slight rattle of the pages betrayed her state of being while he remained so cool and untouched. It seemed so unfair for her to be feeling like a chastised child while he acted the role of the reprimanding authority figure.

'You should read them carefully before you sign them,' he added.

She pulled out her chair and sat down before she realised what she had done. She'd had no intention of taking her seat while he was still sitting but somehow he had got his way. 'Nice one, Vallini,' she said, giving him a narrow-eyed glance.

'Read the document, Rachel,' he said expressionlessly.

She read through the document carefully. It stated that she was to be temporarily employed as his housekeeper and in doing so was required to sign a confidentiality agreement. If she spoke to the press during the time of her employment or for up to six months afterwards she would have to repay all monies paid to her, including the ten thousand euros he had already given her.

'Is there a problem?' Alessandro asked.

She looked across at him, wondering why he was being so calculated about this. It seemed a bit extreme for a two-day stay. But then he had good reason to think she would do anything to get the money she so desperately needed. A quick spill to the press had the potential to earn her thousands but there was no way she would dream of doing that to someone, not after knowing firsthand how it felt to have your private life splashed across every headline. 'No, not really,' she said. 'It seems pretty straightforward. You're paying me to keep my mouth shut.'

'A day or two at the most is all I want from you,' he said. 'Once that time is up you are free to go. You will not owe me a penny unless you act with indiscretion.'

Rachel took the pen, her fingers feeling the warmth of where his had been. He hadn't touched her, not even a brush of his fingers as he handed her the pen, but her hand felt as if it were on fire. She signed her name before handing the pen and the document back to him. 'Do you get all your mistresses to sign confidentiality agreements before you sleep with them?' she asked.

His eyes glinted darkly as they held hers. 'You are not technically being employed as my mistress, Rachel.'

Rachel felt her colour rise. 'How do I know you won't add it to my list of duties?'

He took a long time to answer. A very long time. 'I don't like mixing business with pleasure,' he said. 'It is a dangerous combination that can leave one open to exploitation.'

Rachel knew he was having a dig at her for the way she had led him on in the past. From his point of view she had acted like a trashy little tart, offering herself to him at every opportunity. She had flirted with him and teased him and had enjoyed every moment of it. He had made her feel so feminine and gorgeous and so irresistible that it had gone completely to her head. But looking back now she wished she had been a little more mature and a little more sensible about how she had conducted herself.

Alessandro put the papers to one side and reached for

the bottle of champagne. 'Shall we celebrate our temporary arrangement?' he said.

'Why not?' Rachel said, affecting a carefree tone when she felt anything but.

He handed her a glass of sparkling bubbles and then, taking his own, held it against hers in a toast. 'To standing up for oneself,' he said and drank a hefty mouthful.

She took a small sip and then frowned as she traced the rim of her glass with her fingertip. 'I'm a lot better at it now than I was.'

Alessandro put his glass down. 'I don't know about that. I think you've always been good at fighting from your corner.'

There was a little silence.

'When did you decide to end your relationship with Hughson?' he asked.

She looked at the contents of her glass rather than meet his eyes. 'I could see things were not working out between us,' she said. 'We had very little in common apart from our backgrounds. I think I always knew that but I was under pressure from my father to do the right thing.'

'Meaning he wanted you to marry money.'

His statement sounded like a criticism. 'Yes, but then that was the way I was brought up,' Rachel said. 'I was taught to mix with the right people.'

'But you amused yourself by the occasional fraternisation with the lower classes,' he said.

Rachel met the glacial glitter of his unwavering gaze. 'I can't really explain my behaviour,' she said, looking away again. 'I didn't intend to hurt you. I think I just got carried away. I had spent years insulting you and then I was suddenly fighting an attraction that was beyond anything I had experienced before…'

'So you ended your engagement,' Alessandro said after a pause.

'Yes. I would have broken things off a lot earlier but… but it was hard to…well, to admit I had got it so wrong about him.'

'Pride.'

She looked up at him, her white teeth snagging at her bottom lip in that bewildered-child manner that never failed to stir something deep and primal in him. 'Yes, pride and the fact that my father thought Craig was everything a future son-in-law should be. I called off the wedding twenty-four hours before it was scheduled to go ahead, and my father has never let me forget how it contributed to his bankruptcy. I knew Craig had poured a bit of money into the business but I hadn't realised how much. Of course he subsequently pulled out everything once I called off the wedding. And then there was all that food, all those flowers, the dress, the cake—you can probably imagine how it went.'

'I can.'

She bit her lip again, deeper this time, so deep Alessandro wanted to reach out and brush her soft lip with the pad of his thumb to restore its soft plumpness.

He picked up his glass instead and took another mouthful of the champagne. He didn't want to think about her with her ex-fiancé. He hated thinking about her with that creep. Every day of that liaison had been like a lighted poker to his flesh. It had tortured him to think of her with that brute's hands and mouth and body on hers. But it was what she had chosen. She had chosen Hughson's money over his love. He had been totally gutted by her shallowness and greed. He had fought for years to put it behind him, to keep his emotions in check, to live life without feeling anything for anyone. But now his hatred for what she had done returned with a vengeance. For so long he had ignored it, but now it was back like a filthy choking tide clogging his blood. He hated her with the same passion as with which he had once loved her.

'You never liked him, did you?' she said, looking at him again.

Alessandro put his glass down. 'Are we talking about your father or your fiancé?' he asked.

Twin flags of colour rose in her cheeks. 'Both really…'

'I realise it is never comfortable hearing someone criticise someone you love,' he said. 'But then that is what is so endearing about young children. They only see the good in their parents.'

'I was hardly an infant when you came to work for my father,' she said. 'I was eighteen years old, legally an adult.'

Alessandro pictured her back then, all rich-kid attitude with no idea how the real world worked—the world he had been dragged through for as long as he could remember. Her silver-spoon lifestyle made her feel superior. She had looked down that up-tilted nose of hers and sneered at anyone who wasn't dressed in the latest designer wear or driving the fastest sports car. He had taken it on the chin for the first couple of years, putting up with her catty remarks about his background or his clothes or the second-hand car he drove. But then she had started flirting with him. He had ignored it at first but after a time she had been impossible to resist. The first time he had kissed her his senses had imploded. His body had throbbed and ached for her but he had never pushed her to sleep with him. He hadn't felt comfortable concealing their relationship. He had wanted to go public with it but she had always insisted no one must know. Little had he realised it had all been a game to her; leading him on for weeks on end, only to reject him like a stray mongrel dog that had the audacity to have turned up at a pedigree show. For the last few years he had felt glad she had got her comeuppance. He had watched from a distance as she had lost her modelling contract, and then how the slurs on her reputation were played out in the press, which left her with no one willing to take her on, and he had felt nothing but satisfaction.

She deserved it for how she had treated him. He had been blinded by lust. He felt foolish for having thought he had ever loved her. But then he had loved a fantasy, not a real person. He had fooled himself she was not the selfish, pouting little spitfire she presented to the world, but instead a soft and caring young woman who hadn't felt safe enough in her relationships to reveal her vulnerabilities. But he had got it wrong. She was every bit as selfish and spiteful on the inside as she was on the outside. The fact that she had sought him out for money after all this time and in spite of their history was proof of it.

She had no shame.

Looking at her now, with her beautiful face without its armour of make-up and those incredible eyes shadowed and downcast, he knew he would have to guard against her wiles. She hadn't suddenly morphed into a demure little lady and he wasn't going to treat her like one until she learned how to behave.

Her beautifully manicured hand was toying with the stem of her champagne flute. Alessandro felt a stirring in his groin as he thought of how it would feel to have those soft fingers trace over him, to encircle him, to milk him of his essence. He forced the image out of his head. The doctors kept assuring him it would just take a little more time, but how much time? It had been close to two months now. Two months of doing everything he could to regain what he had lost, to allow his body to heal. But no one had given him any guarantees. No one had said for certain he would regain full mobility and function. Yes, there were positive signs of improvement but what if that was as far as his body would ever go? He was luckier than most. He knew that and was grateful for it but he wanted his life back.

He wanted it more than anything.

Rachel put her fork down when she was finished and noticed Alessandro watching her. 'Is something wrong?' she asked.

His expression was unfathomable. 'No, I was just checking to see if you used the right cutlery.'

Hot colour flooded her cheeks. 'You're never going to forgive me for those little digs about your background, are you?' she said, glaring at him.

He picked up his champagne glass and drained it. The sound of it coming back to the table's starched linen surface was like a thump in the silence. 'You are very prickly, aren't you, *cara*?'

Rachel's heart gave a little squeeze at his casually delivered endearment. Even the way he said her name had a similar effect on her. His accent had deepened over the time he had spent in Italy. His voice was smooth and mellifluous. It was another devastatingly attractive feature of him that unsettled her deeply. How could a man's voice make a woman's spine soften like warmed honey? The deep timbre of Alessandro's voice was like a sensual stroke of a lover's hand. If that was just what his voice could do to her what would happen if he decided to change the rules of their arrangement? 'Why did you call me that?' she asked.

He gave her a brief flash of a smile that didn't involve his eyes. 'Are you still worried I might try and seduce you now I have you within my clutches?'

Rachel had difficulty disguising her reaction to his unnerving mind-reading ability. She quickly got her shocked expression under control, however, and resorted to sarcasm. 'You can try but whether or not you will succeed is another matter entirely.'

This time his smile lasted longer and made the whole distance to his dark blue eyes, the teasing glint making her toes curl inside her shoes. 'Are you laying down a challenge for me, *tesoro mio*?' he asked.

Her fingers fumbled on her glass, almost knocking it over. 'No, of course not,' she said. 'I-I'm not interested in anything like that.'

'You have been single now for how long?' he asked as he refilled her glass.

She hesitated before she answered. She was twenty-six years old and had only had a couple of lovers. Her first experience had been a teenage fumble that had seriously dented her confidence, but sex with Craig had confirmed every fear she'd held about herself. In hindsight she could see she had been too young and inexperienced and too stubborn to accept she had made a mistake in becoming engaged to him. Instead of extricating herself from the relationship she had clung to it all the harder, pretending it was something it was not and never could be.

'Rachel?' Alessandro prompted.

She met his dark eyes. 'I have been pretty busy just lately trying to save my label,' she said. 'There hasn't been a lot of time for socialising.'

'Tell me about your friend,' he said. 'You are business partners, yes?'

'Yes,' Rachel said. 'Caitlyn and I met at design school. We got on well and had similar goals. She was a great support to me when I ended things with Craig. I don't know what I would have done without her. She once had a violent controlling partner so she knew what it was like to...'

Alessandro was very quiet and Rachel looked up to see him studying her with a frowning expression on his face. 'Sorry... I'm rambling,' she said.

'Did Hughson hurt you physically?' he asked, still frowning heavily.

'No, but he made threats,' Rachel said. 'I guess that's how he controlled me for so long. I was never sure what he was capable of. I wasn't game to risk it. I finally got the courage to end things but only because of Caitlyn's help. She showed me how I was being manipulated.' She lowered her gaze from his. 'I was too stupid to see it for myself.'

Alessandro reached across the table and put his hand on her arm. 'Don't blame yourself.'

Rachel felt the slow spreading warmth of his flesh on hers. His skin was so tanned compared to hers. His fingers so long and dusted with masculine hair, the nails clean and short, strong hands, capable hands, hands that could stroke and caress and light fires underneath her skin. She swallowed as a wing-like flutter erupted in her belly. She slowly brought her gaze up to his. It felt as if he had summoned it with the sheer power of his magnetic presence. His pupils were black holes in a dark blue unfathomable sea. It occurred to her then she could drown in that sea if she wasn't careful. 'I guess you must be really pleased I had to lie down on the bed of my own making,' she said.

Alessandro removed his hand from her arm and sat back in his chair. 'I am not sure it is a worthwhile exercise relishing in someone else's misfortune,' he said. 'No one gets it right all the time. I have made decisions I have come to regret in hindsight.'

Rachel could just imagine what he most regretted. Asking her to marry him and then only minutes later to have her introduce another man as her fiancé would surely be up there with the most regrettable of actions. If only he knew how much she wished she had said yes to him instead. Her life would have been so very different.

'I'll get the next course,' she said to break the awkward silence.

While she was in the kitchen she looked down at her arm where his hand had lain and fully expected it to show some mark, so heightened were her senses. Her skin tingled, each nerve prickling beneath the surface of her skin.

She rubbed at her arm, annoyed with herself for reacting like an infatuated schoolgirl instead of a mature and sensible adult. She could not afford to be distracted by his potent allure. She was on a mission to save her label and that had to remain her top and only priority.

Once Rachel had served the meal Alessandro turned the conversation to more neutral topics. It was as if he was making a concerted effort to steer away from any mention of the past. Rachel found him to be a convivial host when he put his mind to it. He asked her what books she had read lately, what movies she had enjoyed and where she had last holidayed. He even laughed at one of her anecdotes about a visit to a celebrity client for a private fitting. Rachel suddenly realised she had never heard him laugh before. It was a deep rich sound that trickled down her spine like a flow of champagne. It was a magical moment, connecting them in a way that she had not experienced with him before. She caught a glimpse of the man he was and had always been in spite of his difficult background: respectful, disciplined, driven but decent. Why had it taken her this long to realise it?

Before she knew it the time had come for coffee.

'Have you been back to Australia since you left?' she asked as she poured them each a cup of the rich fragrant brew.

'No.'

'Why not?'

He stirred his black coffee even though she hadn't seen him put in any sugar. 'It is a good country—a great country,' he said. 'I have never said it wasn't, but my heart is in Italy. As soon as I got off the plane I felt as if I had come home.'

'Your father was Italian, wasn't he?'

'Yes.' He picked up his cup and took a sip. 'He travelled to Australia on a working holiday but ended up staying after he met my mother.'

Rachel had never heard him speak of his parents before. 'So why did you end up in foster homes?' she asked.

His expression was remote. 'My father died in a workplace accident when I was a small child. Things came unstuck after that.'

'Do you remember him?' she asked.

'Yes,' he said. 'He was tall like me and had the same colouring. He worked hard trying to get ahead but he never quite made it. Everything seemed to work against him, including my mother.'

'Is she still alive?' Rachel asked.

'She died a few years ago,' he said. 'I didn't hear about it until the funeral was over.'

'You mean you didn't try to keep in touch with her?'

His eyes met hers, dark, veiled and deep. 'I tried but it

didn't always help matters. In the end I thought it best to keep out of her life.'

'Why was that?' Rachel asked.

'She was totally unreliable,' he said 'She was always changing addresses and or partners, most of whom were her dealers. She was the reason my father had to work three jobs to keep food on the table. She shot most of what he earned up her arms. It was a problem she couldn't fight alone. Once he died she spiralled out of control without him there to support her.'

Rachel's throat constricted. She had always known he had come from a difficult background but she had never bothered to ask how difficult. She had heard rumours that he had been kicked out of numerous foster homes and thus assumed he had always been a rebel of some sort, that *he* was the problem. 'I'm so sorry,' she said, her voice coming out as soft as a whisper. 'I had no idea things had been that bad for you. I thought you were just one of those hard-to-manage kids. You never said anything.'

'My father was a fool for falling in love with my mother,' he said. 'Her first love wasn't him, it was her next high. He should have realised there are some people who are beyond help. He got caught in the addiction web and it cost him his life.'

'It must have been so awful for you having no one to rely on after your father was killed,' Rachel said. 'How did you manage?'

'How does any kid manage?' he said. 'The survival instinct kicks in. I was a bit wild for a time until I made a decision to follow my father's dream of a better life. I got off the streets and got an education.'

'I am sure he would be very proud of you,' Rachel said.

Alessandro gave an indifferent shrug. 'I am not proud of my background but it has made me the man I am today. I suppose I should be grateful, *si*? I could have followed my mother's example. So many people do. It is all they know. It's as if it is somehow programmed into their genes. Generational dysfunction or some such thing it is called.'

'How did you change the cycle when so many can't or won't?'

'I wanted to win, Rachel,' he said with a determined set to his features. 'I have always wanted to win because my father's chance was thrown away.'

'So winning at any cost is important to you?'

His eyes burned a pathway to her soul. 'Very important,' he said. 'I will not stop until I get what I want.'

Rachel picked up her coffee cup for something to do with her hands. She wanted to reach out and lay her hand on his arm as he had done to her earlier but she wasn't sure how it would be interpreted. When it came to that she wasn't sure how *she* would react. Would her touch turn into a caress or a plea for forgiveness or both? Would she slide her hand up and down his hair-roughened arm, maybe even entwine her slim, small fingers with his long, strong ones? Her belly gave another little two-step shuffle and she gripped her coffee cup a little harder, but the cup was hot and somehow she lost her hold, the liquid spilling on the stark whiteness of the tablecloth, some of it splashing against her chest.

'Are you all right?' Alessandro asked. 'You didn't burn yourself, did you?'

'No, I'm fine,' she said, using the napkin he had rapidly handed her to mop up the spillage. 'I'm sorry. I'm not normally so clumsy.'

He remained seated while she cleared the table, which she

tried not to be annoyed about. He was paying her and generously to wait on him. She had no right to feel resentful. If anything she should be bending over backwards to get him to consider backing her label. It was demeaning to be in such a position but she really had no choice. 'Alessandro…' she began, 'I just want to say how much I—'

'Go to bed, Rachel,' he said as if dismissing an overtired child from the adults' dinner table. 'Your work here is finished for the day. We will speak again in the morning.'

'But I—'

'Don't argue with me, Rachel,' he said. 'You are obviously exhausted. I should not have kept you up so late. I'm sorry. I lost track of the time.'

Rachel turned and left, not happy about being dismissed but she realised by the way the shutters came down on his face that he was probably regretting revealing so much about his background. She felt ashamed that she hadn't probed him about it five years ago. Why had she just assumed he was a bad boy? Why hadn't she looked a little closer and understood why he was so driven and determined? He was a man on a mission to succeed and she had been a part of that plan but had defaulted. No wonder he was enjoying watching her taking orders from him.

Success, after all, was the ultimate revenge.

It was only as she was washing her face in preparation for bed that she realised her mother's pendant was missing from around her neck. A tight band of panic wrapped around her insides as she shook out her clothes to see if it had caught on them as she had undressed but there was no sign of it. She then retraced her steps, all over the large bedroom and then back to the en suite, her eyes scouring the floor as she went for the glint of a diamond and the silver of the fine chain, but there was nothing. She spread out the contents of her hand-bag on the bed, going through everything meticulously but still not able to see the pendant anywhere. She checked the sink of the basin she had used, but without the services of a plumber to undo the S-bend she was unable to know for sure if it had slipped down there or not. She bit her lip and thought hard about when she had last felt it around her neck. But because she wore it most of the time she was so used to feeling it there that she *didn't* feel it. It was a part of her that just was…well, a part of her.

And now it was gone.

A choked sob rose in her throat. She couldn't lose it. It was all she had of her mother. She just couldn't possibly lose it. She would tear this wretched villa asunder to find it even if it took her the whole night to do it.

There was a satin robe that Lucia had given her earlier and she wrapped it around herself quickly to continue the search.

She went down the stairs, turning on lights as she went, her eyes on the floor the whole time. She went across the foyer and then down to the dining room and opened the door. The table was as she had left it, shiny and cleared with a vase of roses in the centre filling the room with their scent.

She got on her hands and knees and went over the thick carpet with her hands and strained eyes. She was close to tears by now, her heart sinking at the thought of losing that final link with her mother.

'Oh, dear God, where are you?' she said out loud as she sat back on her heels and pushed the hair out of her face.

Rachel had her back to the door and it took her a moment to shuffle around on her knees in order to identify the sound that had whispered over the thick carpet like a fox on velvet paws.

Her heart swung like a wildly flung anvil in her chest when she saw Alessandro sitting in a wheelchair, his blue-black eyes meeting hers. 'Is this what you are looking for?' he asked, her mother's pendant dangling from his long tanned fingers.

CHAPTER FOUR

RACHEL gulped, her eyes going to the chair and then back to his unflinching gaze. 'I... I...'

He gave her a dispassionate look. 'I am sorry I can't rise in your presence but I am confident that within the next few days I will be able to do so.'

Her face exploded with shame. She felt every single capillary fill with it. 'I had no idea... I'm so sorry... I wish I had known. I would never have said the things... *Oh, God, the awful things I said.*' She bit on her lip so hard she tasted blood. She mentally recalled every insult, every horrible insult she had flung at him for not standing. It had never occurred to her that he couldn't. Oh, dear God, what must he think of her? Emotion clogged her throat, tightening it until she couldn't speak. Every moment she had spent with him he had been sitting, apart from when he had been in the pool, but even there she could not recall him standing. He had leaned against the edge and later had pulled himself out of the water and sat with his legs in the water. Why hadn't he said something? Why hadn't Lucia warned her? What was going on?

Alessandro used his hands to roll the wheelchair towards her. 'You can stand up,' he said. 'I don't expect you to kneel at my feet like a servant from the Dark Ages.'

Rachel scrambled ungainly to her feet, momentarily

forgetting she was dressed in nothing but a slip of satin that was probably showing every contour of her body. It was only as she felt his dark blue gaze run over her that she wished she had asked Lucia for something a little less revealing to wear. 'You found my pendant,' she said unnecessarily.

'Yes.' He handed it to her. 'It must have fallen from your neck when you dabbed at your spilt coffee on your top. It was on the floor. I found it as I was leaving to go upstairs.'

Rachel tried to put the pendant back on but her fingers wouldn't cooperate. She gave it another try but it slipped out of her hands and she had to kneel down again to retrieve it off the floor.

'Here,' he said. 'Allow me.'

She leaned towards him but it brought her so close to his face her breath stalled in her throat.

They were eye to eye.

His eyes were so very dark. His breath was minty and fresh as it caressed her face. She could see the pinpoints of stubble on his jaw, the fresh dark growth triggered by the rush of his potent male hormones. Her fingers ached to feel the rasp of his stubble under her fingertips, to trace the sensual contour of his mouth. Her lips tingled to feel the hard press of his on hers, her heart beat so hard and so fast in anticipation she was sure he could hear it. For that matter *she* could hear it. It was like the roar of the ocean in her ears: pounding, tumultuous, deafening.

Alessandro took the pendant from her fingers and looped it around her neck, one of his hands lifting the curtain of her hair to free it from the snare of the chain. Rachel's skin shivered in reaction, not just her neck but her entire body, inside and out. His touch was like fire. Her skin felt as if it were going to erupt into flames; every nerve ending was fizzing like a child's bonfire-night sparkler.

'There,' he said, leaning back once the catch was secure. 'You should probably get a jeweller to look at it to make sure it doesn't come loose again.'

Rachel fingered the pendant, her eyes still locked on his as if tethered there by some invisible energy source. 'Thank you,' she said in a scratchy-sounding voice. 'I don't know what I would have done if I had lost it.'

'It is obviously very valuable to you.'

'Yes, it was my mother's,' she said, sitting back on her heels. 'It's all I have of hers.'

'Well, at least you have it back now,' he said.

Rachel bit her lip and then dived right in. 'How did it happen?'

He looked at her for a long pause without speaking. She waited with baited breath, wondering if he was weighing up the odds about revealing what had happened to him. Was this why she had been made to sign the confidentiality agreement? Did he think so poorly of her that he had to go to that extreme?

'Have you heard of Guillain-Barré syndrome?' he asked at last.

'Yes, I think so,' she said. 'It's caused by a virus, isn't it?'

'That's correct,' he said. 'About two months ago after a trip abroad I developed a slight chest infection. It was nothing out of the ordinary, or so I thought. A few days later I developed some weakness in my legs. Again, I thought I had just overdone it. I had been training for a marathon before I got sick. But it turned out to be Guillain-Barré. The illness results in the inflammation and destruction of myelin in the peripheral nerves. Sometimes the paralysis can be far more serious when it affects the breathing or the ability to swallow. I am told I am one of the lucky ones. It is only my legs that have been affected, hopefully not permanently.'

Rachel didn't know what to say. She was still reeling from the shock of it all. She was still flaying herself for everything she had said to him. Why hadn't he said something? Surely he hadn't hoped to keep his condition a secret from her while she was here? Or had he deliberately left it as long as he could so she could hang herself with the rope he had so very cleverly fed out to her?

'Don't worry, Rachel,' he said with an embittered look. 'It's not catching.'

She frowned as she realised how he had interpreted her silence. 'I'm not in the least concerned about that.'

One brow rose cynically. 'Are you not?'

'Of course not,' she said.

'So, you're not planning on leaving at first light?' he asked.

'I'm not leaving.' As soon as she said the words she realised how deeply she meant them. He thought her a woman without honour and principles but she would show him just how honourable and principled she had become. She would stand by her agreement with him. She would stay as long as he needed her.

He pushed his chair back from where she was kneeling on the floor. 'I don't want your pity,' he said, biting out each word as if they were something bitter and distasteful.

'I'm not offering you pity,' she said. 'I think it's terrible that you've been dealt this but that's empathy, not pity.'

'Get up off the floor, for God's sake,' he said irritably.

Rachel stood up and brushed the borrowed wrap back down over her thighs. 'Is there anything you need?' she asked. 'Can I help you with anything?'

His dark eyes glittered as they held hers. 'What exactly are you offering, Rachel? Your delectable body to awaken my half-dead nerves?'

Her face suffused with colour all over again. 'That wasn't part of the arrangement,' she said.

'We could make it part.'

Her eyes rounded. 'You can't mean that.'

'I can do what I want, Rachel,' he said. 'I am the one holding the purse strings now, remember?'

'Am I to be punished for every horrible word I ever said to you?' she asked. 'Is that what this is about? You want a whipping boy and I am it?'

His eyes were dark blue chips of ice. 'Go to bed, Rachel. I will see you in the morning.'

'Don't dismiss me like a child,' she said with a late show of her wilfulness. 'You're always doing that. It's so annoying.'

His hands gripped the turning mechanism on his chair. 'Are you determined to see me lose my temper?'

'I'm not scared of you, Alessandro,' Rachel said.

'Then you should be,' he said, fixing her with a searing look. 'I can do more harm to you than ten of your worthless, spineless fiancés. One word from me and your fashion career will be over. No one in the whole of Europe will touch you with a bargepole. Am I making myself clear?'

Rachel swallowed a walnut-sized restriction in her throat. 'If you do that you will not just be destroying me but my business partner too.'

A pulse ticked at the side of his mouth. 'Then you had better behave yourself, hadn't you, *cara*?' he said and, without waiting for a response from her, he turned on his wheels and left.

* * *

Rachel lay in bed much later without any hope of getting to sleep. She had watched the clock go around in fifteen-minute slots, each one seeming slower than the one before. It was now close to dawn. She could see the fingers of sunlight poking through the gap in the curtains, casting the room in an incandescent glow of pink and gold.

Alessandro's threat was still ringing in her ears. He could destroy her with a word. She had no way of knowing whether he would do it or not. He certainly had the motivation to do so. She had no choice but to do everything his way. Failing this time would not just be devastating professionally but personally as well. It would be the confirmation of all of her worst fears that she didn't have the talent and drive to achieve anything in life.

She had heard the whirr and grind of the lift taking Alessandro to his suite of rooms a couple of hours ago. It seemed he too was late to bed. She wondered if he had been to sleep or whether he had tossed and turned as she had done. He had said he hoped to be back on his feet within a few days, but what if it took longer? She wasn't sure what the timeframe of the syndrome was or whether it was different for every person. All she knew was that he was one of the most physically active people she had ever met. The fact that her father had exploited Alessandro's willingness to work so hard had not really occurred to her until later when those very standards had clashed with her own. She hadn't spoken to her father in a couple of years, not since he had asked her to bail him out of yet another gambling disaster. The fact that he had lost everything, including the house and garden her mother had loved so much, destroyed any hope of a continuing relationship with him. He would have pawned her mother's pendant if she hadn't caught him just in time.

She threw back the covers and wandered over to the window, pulling back the curtains with the beaded chain hanging by the side. The pool below was sparkling invitingly. Before she could change her mind she put on her rinsed out bra and knickers, and, wrapping her body in a bath sheet as a sarong, went down the marble staircase to the door that led out to the terrace.

She slipped into the water and practised her strokes. It was a beautiful morning, warm already with a promise of later heat. The water was a perfect temperature and she turned onto her back, closing her eyes as she floated...

Alessandro frowned as he read the email from Sheikh Almeed Khaled. The sheikh requested Alessandro bring his current partner to a private dinner at his luxury hotel in Paris the following week. There would be follow-up meetings during the week, but to meet privately was a good sign the sheikh was moving closer to sealing the deal. However, the invitation presented Alessandro with a problem. Turning up without a partner for the dinner, let alone the week, could make the sheikh suspicious that all was not well with him. He had seen deals brokered and lost before on the whisper of an illness. The business world he moved in was ruthless. People did not make allowances for personal issues. It was cut-throat and heartless but that was the way things worked. A deal was a deal.

He turned away from the computer to look out of the window, his brain ticking over the best way to handle the situation, when he caught sight of the miscreant mermaid floating in his pool in the early morning light. The sun had painted her slim body in an ethereal glow, her hair streaming out behind her in silken strands. He drummed his fingers on the arms of his chair as he thought of how he could work things to his advantage.

Rachel needed money.

He needed a temporary mistress.

Like all the other women in his life she would serve her purpose for the allotted time but that would be the end of it. His relationships were just like any other business transaction. Both parties teamed up for a specified time and parted with what they had agreed on at the outset. The rest of the month with Rachel would prove to him he was able to walk away without a single pang of regret.

He would feel nothing.

Zip.

Nada.

Niente.

He smiled as he made his way down to the pool. This was going to be far more entertaining that he had first thought.

Rachel turned over and saw him by the pool, her sea-glass eyes blinking the water out as she stood and shielded her lace-covered breasts with her hands. 'I—I didn't hear you,' she said.

Alessandro gave her a semblance of a smile as he tapped the wheels with his hands. 'It's the deluxe model,' he said, 'streamlined and stealthy.'

She bit her lip in that childlike way of hers that undid him every time. He would have to work harder at covering it, at conquering it. She was not a guileless child. She never had been. She was a manipulating, down-on-her-luck gold-digger. She had already sold herself once. She would do it again. It would be amusing to watch her game play this time around.

'I'll get out to give you some more room,' she said, and moved towards the side of the pool.

'I am sure there is room in there for the two of us,' Alessandro said.

She stalled with her hands on the rails that led from the steps. 'I just thought you might like some privacy.'

He sent his eyes over her slim form, taking his time over the upthrust of her breasts before he met her gaze. He felt the stab of lust deep in his groin, his body springing to life, aching, pulsing, filling and lengthening. 'If anyone deserves some privacy it is you,' he said, keeping his expression dead-pan. 'Hopefully the rest of your luggage will arrive within the next twenty-four hours.'

'I didn't think you would be down here this early,' she said. 'I had a bad night. I couldn't sleep. I thought some exercise would help.'

He moved his chair closer to the pool. 'It's a great panacea for many ills.'

He was conscious of her watching him as he manoeuvred himself from the chair to the railing of the pool steps. He was able to take a couple of steps, which was better than even twenty-four hours ago. It spurred him on to work harder and harder at his exercises.

He *would* beat this.

He refused to consider any other alternative.

He swam a couple of lengths to loosen up his muscles and came back to where she was still standing, holding the rails of the steps. 'I haven't contaminated the water, you know,' he said.

She frowned at him. 'I wish you wouldn't immediately as-sume the worst of me.'

'Swim with me, then,' he said. 'We can train together. I

could do with the company. It gets pretty boring going up and down by oneself.'

She stepped back down into the water. 'You're very good at this, swimming, I mean,' she said. 'No one would ever think that you… I mean…'

'Half a man?' he said.

'I never said that,' she said. 'I never even thought it.'

'It's what most people think.'

'I'm not most people,' she said. 'I know you think I'm spoilt and shallow and I was before. I freely admit that. But the last few years have changed me. I don't judge people on appearances or what they lack in terms of background or breeding. We are all the same on this earth. Everyone is equal.'

He gave a snort of derision. 'You expect me to believe you have reinvented yourself? You haven't got a clue how the other half lives, Rachel. You have never had to beg for a meal. You have never had to sleep rough when the cold creeps into your bones until you can barely move the next morning. You have never had to fight off predators who want your soul for the price of their next fix.'

His words seemed to hit her like physical blows and he instantly regretted revealing so much of his sordid past. As soon as he had done it last night he had wished he hadn't. She could so easily use it against him. He'd had plenty of opportunities to tell her five years ago but he'd always held back. He hadn't wanted to sully their budding relationship with the dark shadows of his past. He realised now part of her allure back then had been that air of sassy innocence she had perfected.

She bit her lip again. He saw the way her teeth pushed the blood away until her lip turned almost bone-white, and then how when she released it the blood flooded back, making her lips cherry-red. Damn it, why did she keep doing that?

'I think I'll go inside and shower,' she said, moving back to the steps.

'Rachel.'

She stopped and turned to look at him. 'Yes?'

'I have a proposition for you,' Alessandro said.

She looked at him warily. 'You do?'

'I have decided to give you the backing you need,' he said.

A gleam of excitement shone in her eyes. 'You have?'

'But I want something in return.'

The excitement faded. 'Which is?' she asked.

He nailed her with his eyes. 'I want you to be my mistress for the rest of the month.'

Her eyes went wide and her cheeks flushed. 'P-pardon?'

Alessandro smiled. *Dio*, she was good at playing the game. So coy, so convincing. 'You heard.'

'I'm sorry, but for a moment there I thought you said you want me to be your mistress.' She gave her head a little shake. 'I must have water in my ears.'

Alessandro waited for a beat. 'I am willing to fully back your label as well as pay you generously for each day of our time together.'

Her expression tightened, her eyes narrowing in anger. 'I knew you would do this. I knew you would change the rules to suit yourself.'

'Whether you sleep with me will be entirely up to you,' he said. 'It is not a condition on the deal.'

She faltered for a moment, a frown pulling at her smooth brow. 'I… I don't understand… You just said you would pay me to be your mistress…'

'In public, not necessarily in private,' Alessandro said.

Her frown deepened. 'You want me to *act* as if I'm your mistress?'

'I am sure you can do it convincingly,' he said. 'After all, you have done it before, *si*?'

Her mouth flattened in anger. 'Do you have any idea of how much I hate you for doing this?'

'Right back at you, little rich girl,' he said.

She got out of the pool and snatched up her towel. 'You expect me to say yes, don't you?' she said.

'I expect you to think carefully before you throw away your only lifeline,' he said.

She gave him a look that would have cut through a diamond. 'Let me get back to you on that,' she said.

'I have so far managed to keep the news of my affliction out of the press,' he said. 'I realise that will be impossible if I am not able to regain my full mobility over the next few weeks, but I refuse to accept that outcome. I can now manage a few steps with support. My goal is to move to crutches in the next couple of days. That will make being seen in public a lot less complicated and no one will blink an eye about it. I will explain it as a sprain or something. You read and signed the disclosure contract. Do I have to remind you of the consequences of not playing by the rules?'

'Do you think so badly of me that you think I would do something like that?' she asked.

'I will have another contract drawn up ready for you to sign this evening,' he said.

'And if I don't sign it?'

Alessandro smiled an indolent smile. 'You will sign it, Rachel.'

'Your confidence is admirable but I am not for sale,' she

said with an icy look. 'I will look at other options before I sink that low.'

'You will sign it because you have no choice,' he said. 'Not unless you want to go begging on the streets for your next meal.'

'Aren't you forgetting something? I can't go out in public with you without clothes.'

'Do not worry, *cara*,' he said. 'I will make sure your luggage is delivered to the door today.'

'And if it isn't?'

'Then I will pay for new clothes for you,' he said.

She glowered at him resentfully. 'I don't want to owe you any more than I have to.'

'You were the one who came to me, Rachel,' he reminded her. 'You are here now and who knows? Perhaps we might even be friends at the end of it.'

'You have a very strange way of recruiting friends,' she tossed back.

Alessandro watched as she wrapped the towel around her body and flounced off. The red-hot blood of desire thundered in his veins, filling him, making him ache with a need that refused to go away. He wanted her more than he had wanted any woman. He wanted her more now than he had five years ago. It was burning like an inferno inside him; day and night it was all he could think about. How much he longed to surge inside her, claiming her as his own, showing her the pleasures of the fiery chemistry that had always been there between them. If it was more money she wanted in exchange for her body, then he would give it. He would part with a fortune to have his fill of her.

But he would still let her go at the end of it.

* * *

Rachel stormed into the shower, turning the water on full, her anger at Alessandro practically bursting through the pores of her skin. Had he planned this right from the start? Of course he had. He had lured her here to play his petty little power games with her. This was a masterstroke at payback. He couldn't have planned a better move. He knew she couldn't say no. Not unless she was prepared to lose everything, including all that Caitlyn had put into the company. How would she be able to face her staff and tell them it was over? She couldn't do it. And Alessandro knew it and was humiliating her with it.

She had not long got out of the shower when he called her on the extension in her room. Her luggage had finally been located and was being delivered within a couple of hours. She marvelled that a single phone call from him had achieved what several from her had not. It was another reminder of the power he had at his fingertips. Power he could use to break her if he chose to.

'I have some work to do so I would like to be left undisturbed until lunch, which I would like served at one,' Alessandro said. 'I hope you can find something to do to occupy your time.'

'I'm sure I can find a doorknob or two to polish,' Rachel said tartly.

'Lucia is returning in the morning so your duties as a housekeeper will cease from midnight tonight,' he said. 'I have told her you will be staying on till the end of the month.'

'I haven't said I would do it yet,' she reminded him.

He ignored her statement as he continued, 'Lucia is also aware that our relationship is not like my usual ones.'

'What? You mean you don't usually blackmail your other women into doing whatever you want?' she shot back.

'I have not had to resort to such means in the past,' he said. 'Most women are perfectly happy with the fringe benefits of sharing my life for a specified time.'

'How can you specify the duration of a relationship?' she asked incredulously. 'Do you have some sort of reminder in your calendar in case you accidentally run over a couple of days? Beep. Time's up. Out you go. Next please.'

'You need have no fear of that happening with us, Rachel,' he said. 'You will be back on that plane to Australia on the first of next month. I can guarantee it.'

He ended the call with an abruptness Rachel found intensely irritating. He was reminding her of her tenuous position here as little more than a servant. It was all part of his mission to extract revenge for the choice she had made, a choice that if she'd had her time over again she would have made so very differently. She put the phone extension back in its cradle and thought back to the night of her twenty-first birthday party…

The mansion was filling with guests for the black-tie affair. Rachel had taken great care over her appearance and was putting on the last touches to her make-up when her father came to see her.

'Rachel, I need a word with you,' he said, looking uneasy.

'Sure,' she said, putting down her tube of lipstick. 'What it is, Dad?'

He pulled at the collar of his dress shirt as if it were strangling him. 'Honey, I need to ask you for a favour, a big one,' he said.

'If you want me to dance with that geeky guy Albert from your firm, forget it,' she said, picking up her lipstick again.

'I can't stand his fleshy hands all over me. He did that at the staff Christmas party and I—'

'Craig has asked for your hand in marriage.'

Rachel looked at her father. 'Shouldn't he have asked *me* first?'

'I guess he didn't see the necessity,' he said. 'You've both always known you would eventually make a go of it. Your mother and I talked of it when you were kids. His parents Kate and Bill wanted it too. They still want it. Now seems the right time to announce it publicly.'

Rachel put a hand to the diamond pendant around her neck that her father had given her only that morning. Her mother had been given it on her twenty-first birthday. She had been wearing it the day she died. 'Dad, there's something I've been meaning to tell you—'

'Craig has invested in my business,' her father cut her off. 'He's really going places, Rachel. He can set you up. He has connections in a modelling agency. They will take you on straight away with just a word from him. You'll travel the world: Paris, London, New York. You'll become a household name.'

'But I'm not in love with him,' Rachel said. 'I thought I was once, when we were teenagers, but not now.'

'Do you think I loved your mother?' her father said through tight lips. 'Don't get me wrong. She was a nice girl but that was the point. I had to marry a nice girl. Not one from the wrong side of the tracks. There are women you sleep with and there are women you marry. It's the same for young women like you born to wealth. You can have your flings if you must, but you have to marry well. You have to marry your own kind. It's a fact of life.'

'But I'm not ready to settle down just yet,' she said. 'I need more time to make up my mind.'

Her father frowned blackly. 'What's this talk of making up your mind? You've always known Craig was the one.'

Rachel swallowed. 'I've just started seeing someone…'

'Who?' The word came out like a bullet.

She felt her stomach begin to churn at the dark threatening look in her father's eyes. 'Alessandro,' she said.

Her father's face turned puce. *The yard boy?*

'He's not just a yard boy,' Rachel said. 'He's doing a business degree, an MBA in fact. He only continues to work here to pay his university tuition.'

'He's trailer trash,' her father said, spittle forming at the side of his mouth. 'He's a mongrel, a crossbreed. For God's sake, he doesn't have a penny to his name!'

'He treats me like a princess,' Rachel said. 'He treats me with respect even though I've been awful to him in the past. I'm just starting to get to know him and I think he's one of the nicest—'

'Are you a complete fool?' he said, his eyes bulging with disgust and scorn. 'You're being used, Rachel, and you're too stupid to see it. He's using you to get ahead. By hooking up with you he gets access to the high-flyers. If you were a poor girl from the suburbs he wouldn't look twice at you.'

Rachel stared at her father open-mouthed. Was it true? Had Alessandro targeted her as his ticket to the big time? They had only been dating a few weeks. She had insisted on keeping their relationship private but he hadn't had the same misgivings. He had wanted to make it public right from the start, he had said he had nothing to be ashamed of in seeing her, but then why would he if what her father had said was true?

'He'll drag you down to the gutter where he came from,'

her father continued. 'I'm warning you, Rachel. If you don't accept Craig's offer of marriage then you will be cut out of my life. I will never speak to you again. Do you hear me?'

Rachel looked at her father in wounded shock. Did he mean it? Did he love her so little that he could cast her from his life without a single slice of regret? Could she risk it? She had already lost her mother. She would have no one if her father cut her off.

'I am sending Craig upstairs as soon as he arrives,' her father went on. 'I want you to come downstairs together as an engaged couple. This is your chance to do something for me, to make me proud. God knows you've given me little to be proud of so far. But this will change everything. I will be the proudest father alive to see you settled with Craig Hughson.'

Rachel's heart sank as her father left the room. The knock on her door a few minutes later made her heart sink even further but, when she opened it, it wasn't Craig standing there, but Alessandro.

She said the first thing that came into her head. 'How did you get in? My father has a security team down there to keep out gatecrashers.'

'I know one of the security guards,' Alessandro said with a flash of his heart-stopping smile.

She closed the door of her bedroom and leaned back against it for support, her eyes avoiding his. 'You can't be here, Alessandro,' she said. 'Not tonight.'

'I wanted to see you on your birthday,' he said. 'I have something I want to ask you.'

She looked at the small velvet package he was holding in one hand. 'I can't take that.' She moved past him to stand in front of the dressing table. She gripped the back of the chair until her knuckles looked as if they would break through her skin.

He came over and, turning her gently, took one of her hands and closed her fingers over the package. 'Rachel,' he said. 'I know we've only been officially dating a few weeks but we've known each other for much longer than that.'

Rachel swallowed as she saw the sincerity in his dark blue gaze as it caught and held hers. 'Don't,' she choked. *Please don't.*

His hands squeezed hers gently. 'I love you,' he said, smiling down at her. 'I think I fell in love with you the first day I came to work here and you insulted me about my manners or my hair, or was it my clothes? It doesn't matter. I love you and I want to marry you. Will you do me the honour of being my wife?'

She tried to get her voice to work but her lips felt as if they were starched. 'Alessandro... I...'

There was a loud knock on Rachel's bedroom door and before she could open her mouth Craig Hughson came in as if he had every right to.

He took in the little tableau with a sneering look. 'What's he doing here?' he asked Rachel.

She couldn't look at Alessandro but she could feel the pressing weight of his gaze. 'He's just leaving,' she said. 'He just wanted to wish me a happy birthday.'

'Well, you can congratulate us while you're at it, Vallini,' Craig said, slinging an arm around Rachel's shoulders.

Alessandro's expression turned to stone. 'Congratulate you on what?'

'Rachel and I are engaged,' Craig said with a smug smile. 'We're just going downstairs to announce it now. Aren't we, babe?'

'Is that true?' Alessandro asked, firing the question at Rachel, his eyes like laser beams.

Rachel wanted to deny it. She ached to deny it. She thought of her father waiting downstairs with all the guests, all the celebrities and high-flyers of Melbourne society, all the well-to-do family friends. They were all assembled waiting for her and Craig to appear. Her father had probably primed them all. They probably had champagne glasses filled and ready for the first congratulatory toast. Could she go down there and say she wouldn't do it, that she wouldn't accept Craig's offer of marriage? She had no home but this one. No other relative but her father. How could she cut herself off from all that was familiar to take a chance on a relationship that was only in its infancy? She wasn't sure if what she felt for Alessandro was love. It felt like it but how could she know for sure? What if he was asking her to marry him to get ahead in life as her father had implied? She would be better marrying the devil she knew than the one she didn't.

'Is it true?' Alessandro repeated his question, each word enunciated with lethal precision.

Rachel schooled her features into the haughty mask she had used so many times to disguise her true feelings. 'Yes, it's true,' she said. She gave Craig a tight smile and linked her arm through his. 'We're getting married.'

Alessandro didn't say a word. He didn't need to. His anger was a palpable force. It was like a vibration in the room, invisible sound waves of fury. He gave Rachel a look of savage contempt before he moved past, closing the bedroom door with a snap that was as final as a punctuation mark.

Rachel blinked herself out of the past. She didn't want to think about her shameful, cowardly behaviour. She didn't

want to think of the two years of hell with Craig, how he had
cheated on her the whole time they had been together, how he
had borrowed money in her name, falsifying her signature,
leaving her up to the eyeballs in debt and her reputation in
ruins. She didn't want to think about the life she could have
had with Alessandro. She might not have been in love with
him at the time but she hadn't been far off it. Now he hated
her and he had every right to.

The villa was blissfully quiet. Rachel was used to a busy
crowded workspace, people bustling about as she tried to get
everything done that needed to be done. It was amazingly
liberating to be left alone with just her thoughts for company,
and not just her thoughts, but her creative energy. She found
her mind suddenly buzzing with new designs, elegant, sophisticated and inspired by her exotic surroundings. She took
out her sketchbook and drew some outlines, using quick fluid
strokes that captured the essence of what she wanted to pro-
duce for her next collection, barely stopping until thirst and
an aching gnaw in her stomach reminded her it was time to
prepare lunch.

Once the meal was set up, this time on a shady part of the
terrace, she went in search of Alessandro. He wasn't in his
study or in any of the sitting rooms. The pool was empty, for
she had checked it as she had laid the outdoor setting on the
terrace.

She walked past a room on the lower level that she hadn't
seen before. She opened the door without knocking. In one
quick glance she could see the room was a gym. And then
her eyes went to Alessandro, who was on some type of rehabilitation walking frame, beads of sweat on his brow as he
forced one leg in front of the other. It looked as if every step

were a marathon. His mouth was set in a grimly determined line, every muscle in his arms bunched and quivering as they tried to hold his weight as he moved along the short distance across the floor.

Rachel hadn't been aware of making a sound but she must have because he suddenly looked her way and growled at her, his expression savage, like a snarling dog. 'Get out. Get the hell out of here!'

Her hand fell to her side, her chest feeling tight and restricted. 'I'm sorry... I thought you wanted lunch at one...'

He gave her a cutting look. 'I'm not hungry. Now leave.'

She swallowed convulsively as she took in the equipment surrounding him. Weight machines and bench presses, a treadmill that she suspected he hadn't used in a while. All of it a reminder of what he had once been and might never be again. She had secretly admired the sculptured perfection of his muscles all those years ago. She had secretly admired him and compared him to the other men in her life: Craig, who was handsome but lacked definition, her father, who after years of excessive drinking and lack of exercise had become a bloated effigy of the striking-looking man he had once been. Alessandro had surpassed them easily; he always had. His touch had lingered like a memory in her flesh, catching her off guard, taking her by surprise, alerting her to the chemistry that simmered underneath the history of their tricky relationship.

'I told you to get out, Rachel,' he said, his mouth still flat and tight.

'That looks like hard work,' she said, refusing to be daunted, even though her legs were feeling as trembling and unsteady as his seemed to be.

His eyes darkened to midnight blue. 'It is and I would rather not have an audience.'

She moved across to where a pulley with weights attached was hanging from a machine. 'What's this for?' she asked, touching it experimentally.

She heard him draw in a harsh breath behind her. 'It's to maintain my upper body strength,' he said.

She moved to the leg press machine, running a finger over the smooth shiny metal. 'And this?' she asked.

She heard him swear in Italian, a short sharp expletive that for some reason sent a trickling feeling to the base of her spine. Her mind exploded with erotic images of him making love to her, his body strong and in control, pumping, thrusting, filling her with his male presence, stretching her, taking her to the heights of human pleasure. Her face coloured as she realised where her thoughts were taking her.

'I've never seen anyone get hot and sweaty before from just looking at gym equipment,' Alessandro said drily.

Rachel turned away to inspect the hand weights, desperately hoping her colour would subside. She picked up the lightest pair of weights and did a couple of bicep curls. 'I've never really got into the gym thing,' she said. 'I have friends who do several sessions a week. They get antsy if they don't go. It's like an addiction.'

'There are worse things to be addicted to.'

She put the weights down and turned and looked at him again. 'Yes, I suppose so…'

He was studying her, the hard angry look replaced now with a guarded one. 'So what do you do to keep so trim and slim?' he asked. 'Hot and sweaty sessions with your latest lover?'

Rachel felt her face flame again. 'I told you I've been too

busy working on my label. I haven't dated in a while. Actually, not since I broke off my engagement.'

His eyes registered her statement with a tiny flicker of surprise but then he covered it quickly. His voice when he spoke was cynical. 'I somehow can't picture you as a born-again virgin, Rachel. You were always starving for male attention. It didn't matter who they were as long as you could get their notice. I fell for it and I can imagine many have done so since, more fool them.'

'You're never going to let it go, are you?' she said.

His expression remained coolly calm, detached. 'I suppose you are referring to my rather clumsy marriage proposal.'

Rachel's heart was thudding as if she had just done a triple circuit of the equipment in the room with a half marathon thrown in as well. 'I wasn't expecting you to…to—'

'To what?' He cut her off almost savagely, his eyes blazing again. 'To admit I loved you?'

She tugged at her bottom lip with her teeth. 'I was surprised, that's all. I didn't think people fell in love that quickly, or at least not men.'

He gave a grunt of derision. 'I didn't love you, Rachel,' he said. 'I was in lust with you, just like every other man who came within a bull's roar of you. Didn't your father tell you that about men? There are woman you love and there are women you lust after. You are the latter. You will always be the latter.'

Rachel knew her eyes, not to mention her expression, were probably showing much more than she would have liked. Had anyone ever truly loved her? Was it really true that Alessandro had only lusted after her and never seen her for the person she really was? It felt as if a wound inside her had been roughly opened up, exposed and seeping and bleeding all over again.

Her father's words about not loving her mother had haunted her for years. How could men be so cold and calculated about relationships?

'Then why did you want to marry me?' she asked after a short tense silence.

He gave her a look that more or less said it all. 'You were my ticket to success,' he said. 'Marriage to you would have instantly elevated me to the higher echelons of society that had previously been denied me because of my less than desirable background.'

She fought hard to cover her hurt, her devastation, her disappointment that yet again some ruthless, unprincipled man had decided she was to be used as a means to an end. 'But you made it without me,' she said, thinking out loud. 'You didn't need me to achieve what you've achieved.'

He gave her a grim smile of satisfaction. 'I did indeed make it without you, Rachel. I did indeed.'

She moistened her lips again, the cotton wool dryness making her feel slightly ill. 'So why am I here now?'

'Why do you think you are here now?'

She took an unsteady breath, not sure how to respond. She felt as if her world had tipped upside down and she had no way of righting it. 'This is all about revenge, isn't it?' she said.

He gave her a veiled smile. 'What possible way could I have revenge on you?' he asked. 'You are beautiful, you are talented, and you are on the pathway to the pinnacle of brilliant success.'

'As long as I do what you say,' she put in resentfully.

'That is entirely up to you,' he said, and turned back to the equipment. 'I am not forcing you to do anything. I am prepared to back you but only as long as you play the role of my current mistress.'

'What do you want me to do?' she said.

'Just be yourself,' he said, and, clutching the rails, began forcing his legs into action.

She frowned as he moved along the short distance, each leg looking as if it were dragging a road train behind it. The beads of sweat broke out above his top lip and across his brow, and the muscles of his arms bulged with the effort of keeping himself upright. His legs moved inch by inch but it looked as if it took an enormous effort. He gritted his teeth and soldiered on, his eyes narrowed in determination.

'Are you sure you should be trying so hard so soon?' Rachel said. 'Shouldn't you be taking smaller steps or something?'

He looked up at her at that point, his expression caustic. 'I don't need your advice, Rachel. I have a team of physical therapists who help me with this. I have a programme I work through each day. Please leave me to get on with this. I don't want you here.'

She took a step backwards and somehow lost her footing, tumbling over the bench press behind her, landing in a crumpled heap, arms and legs akimbo.

Alessandro swore again, in English this time, and limped over to help her, using the cable skier nearby for support. 'Are you all right?' he said, hauling her to her feet with one of his strongly muscled arms.

It was a precarious rescue. Rachel was not quite upright and nor was Alessandro. His arms were strong but his legs were not. Her arms and legs were rendered useless as soon as he touched her. She turned to jelly, none of her ligaments and muscles seemed to be responding to the messages firing from her brain. She brought him back down with her, the hard weight of his body pinning her to the floor, from thigh to thigh, from pelvis to pelvis.

There was an infinitesimal moment when his eyes locked on hers, their bodies still in an erotic embrace that should have felt awkward and compromising but somehow didn't…

CHAPTER FIVE

RACHEL looked at Alessandro's mouth, the mouth that five years ago had pressed down on hers and evoked a lightning strike of reaction through her being. Her heart raced with a galloping beat, its hammer blows so hard she wondered how he couldn't feel them against his chest where it was pressed against hers. His lips were slightly dry, she could see the indentations of each and every contour, the way the top lip was marginally thinner but the lower one full and sensual—so different from hers, which were evenly full. Hers were soft from years of lip balm and gloss. She had no rough contours, but she knew her smoothness would snare his roughness like hand-spun silk against rough sandpaper. She remembered how it had felt way back then, the difference between their lips startling her, rocking her off course. She felt it again as soon as he touched down, his lips covering hers in a kiss that sent swift sharp shooting arrows of sensation through her. His crushing mouth ensnared hers, capturing her, tethering her in a kiss that was hot and erotic and charged with red-hot passion. She felt it in the way his body was lying over hers. His chest was pressing her down, his pectoral muscles branding her breasts, his taut abdomen imprinting her belly with his unmistakable arousal. She felt the proud swell of his erection, the thundering pulse of his blood, the surge of his hormones awakening every feminine pore of her body.

She felt a pulse of longing start up deep inside her, a throbbing need that escalated with every movement of his mouth on hers until it totally consumed her. When his tongue demanded entry through the tender shield of her lips her pulse skyrocketed. She felt the hot spikes of longing jabbing at her, making her shift beneath him, her body aching for the intimate closeness of his full possession. A fiery pit of need roared inside her core, making her spine arch to feel him right where she needed him most. It was shameful the way she was almost begging, but she couldn't seem to help it. He had awakened a torrent of need inside her that, now unleashed, was racing away with a will of its own. She clawed at him with her greedy hands, holding him to her, her fingers digging into the tautness of his buttocks, pressing him to her aching point of need. His kiss intensified, hot and hard and urgent, even more demanding, his tongue duelling with hers in a passionate showdown that left her breathless and desperate for more. She felt the nip of his teeth as they snagged the fullness of her bottom lip, a shockingly primitive caress that made her spine loosen and her toes curl. She used her teeth the same way on him, spurred on by an instinct as old as time itself, taking his lip, sucking on it, pulling on it, and biting it in little kitten-like bites that evoked a deep throaty groan from him.

He raised his mouth from hers and looked down at her with an expression she couldn't quite read, but at least she could hear his breathing was just about as unsteady as hers. 'Same old Rachel,' he said.

Rachel felt an earthquake of resentment rattle her. 'What do you mean by that exactly?' she asked.

His eyes flicked to her kiss-swollen mouth before coming back to her fiery gaze. 'You are never happy until you have a man under your control, are you?' he said. 'It amuses you to see how readily they succumb to the temptation of your body.'

She gritted her teeth. 'Get off me.'

He gave her a wry smile. 'That's not what you were communicating a couple of minutes ago—the very opposite, in fact.'

'Well, it's what I'm communicating now,' she said and wriggled out from under him to get to her feet.

He propped himself up on one elbow to look at her trying to restore some order to her hair and rumpled clothing. She turned her back on him, furious at how he had made her feel like a cheap strumpet when he had been the one to kiss her first…or had he? She didn't like to think about it too closely. Their mouths had been so close, just a breath apart, and then someone had closed the distance. Had it been him or her or both of them at exactly the same time? His kiss should not have affected her so much. His body should not have left hers aching and crawling with need. She crossed her arms over her body, hoping the action would quell the storm that was still raging inside her. Her skin felt tingling and too sensitive, her breasts tight and full, her inner core moist and hungry for the urgent glide of his flesh in hers. How had he reduced her to this? She turned into a wanton every time he came near her. In spite of the years that had passed nothing had changed.

'This is your bargaining tool, isn't it?' he said. 'You want more money and this is the only way you know how to get it.'

Rachel refused to look at him. 'You think you have this all

sewn up but I could still walk away. There are other people I could approach to help me.'

There was a beat of silence.

'I have been doing a little research into your company,' he said.

Rachel turned around to face him. 'Don't play games with me, Alessandro.'

'The thing is, Rachel, I am very much afraid you will not be able to find anyone else to help you,' he said.

She threw him a cutting glare. 'Because you made sure of it by telling everyone I was a risk.'

'I am not responsible for that, Rachel,' he said. 'You'll have to take my word for it. I am in the process of trying to find out who is, however.'

Rachel didn't believe him for a second. Of course he had blackened her name and reputation. It served his ends to do so.

'The reason I want you to be my counterfeit mistress is because I think you are perfect for the role,' he said. 'You are unlikely to get emotionally involved during the short time of our arrangement. I don't want any complications.'

'Well, that is certainly one thing you've got right,' Rachel said tightly. 'I can assure you there is absolutely no danger of me developing any feelings for you.'

His lips curved upwards in a sardonic smile. 'Still a little too rough for your tastes, little rich girl?'

She glared at him venomously. 'You are a cold, calculating bastard.'

'And you are a stuck-up tease who thinks your body can buy you anything you want,' he shot back with a flash of anger in his eyes.

Rachel stood her ground. She felt strangely invigorated by

their verbal battle of wills. He had always been so amenable in the past. The clash of his will against hers was a new experience, an exhilarating experience. 'You don't have any idea of who I am any more, Alessandro,' she said.

'Some leopards never change their spots,' he said. 'I have met your type time and time again since I left Australia. Women like you are always out for what you can get. People are nothing but instruments to get your own way.'

'But I am not doing this just for myself!' she protested. 'I'm doing it for my friend.'

He gave her a cynical look. 'You are trying to save your company, not your friend. You want to prove to your father that you can make it on your own. You want his approval. You crave it. Your company falling over terrifies you because success is your only means to show him you are not just a beautiful face.'

Rachel swallowed back her retort. She felt stung by his assessment of her motives, not because he was wrong but more because there was an element of truth about what he had observed. All her life she had tried to please her father, to be the sort of daughter he would be proud of, but she had never quite achieved it. She had worked hard at school but she had never gained the results he had in his day. He had constantly reminded her of it. He had been a scholarship student; she had not even been appointed a prefect, let alone Head Prefect or School Captain as he had been. But she resented Alessandro for thinking her support of Caitlyn wasn't genuine. It was. Caitlyn had helped her through her nasty break up with Craig, providing a safe haven when things had got ugly. She had never forgotten the support and friendship her friend had provided.

'What you have to realise, Rachel,' Alessandro continued,

'is you will never please your father. It wouldn't matter if your label became the most successful in the world, it would not make him proud of you. He is a narcissist. He is only interested in what makes him look good. Any success or achievement of yours or anyone else makes him feel resentful, that in some way you or they are deliberately stealing the limelight from her.'

'I don't need my father's approval,' Rachel said. 'I just want to make my own way in the world. I have talent, I know I have. I just need to get things off the ground in Europe.'

'With my help you can take on the world,' he said. 'Is it a deal?'

Rachel looked at him narrowly. 'You said a counterfeit mistress.'

'That is correct.'

'So I really don't have to sleep with you?'

'Not unless you wish to,' he said with a glinting look.

Rachel felt a blush rise in her cheeks. 'What exactly do you get out of this deal?'

'I will make sure I am adequately compensated,' he said. 'I will take a share of the profits on a percentage that is acceptable to us both.'

'It sounds too good to be true, which usually means it is,' she said.

'You're not going to get another offer, Rachel,' he said. 'You'd be wise to take this and make the best of it.'

'You must know I can't possibly say no,' she said.

'You would be a fool indeed to say no,' he said. 'I will still need to analyse your company structure. If I want to instigate changes then you will have to agree to them.'

'I guess I don't have much choice.'

'I have already set up a meeting for you with one of the

top fabric suppliers in the industry,' he said. 'He will be here later tomorrow.'

'Shouldn't I be going to him?' Rachel asked, frowning.

'I am conducting all business from here at the moment,' he said. 'Now, please leave me while I finish my exercises.'

Rachel moved towards the door, but then she stopped and turned around to look at him again. 'Doesn't anyone other than your staff know you have been ill?' she asked.

His sapphire-blue eyes hardened. 'No, and that is the way I want to keep it.'

'But it might take months to get back on your feet. You run a huge corporation. Won't people start to wonder what's going on if you don't turn up to meetings and the like?'

'The beauty of being the boss of a huge corporation is that I get to choose what meetings I go to and when,' he said, reaching for a towel. 'I have a very capable board of directors who run things for me in my absence. But I do not plan to be out of action too much longer. In fact, I have an important meeting next week in Paris. I would like you to accompany me as my mistress. We will be away the whole week. It will be your first major public performance.'

Rachel thought of a week in Paris, pretending to be his mistress. She would be following a long line of women who had probably done the same, although they had been for real. 'I heard about your last mistress,' she said, 'the cosmetics model? She was pretty stunning. Did she know about your illness?'

He tossed the towel to one side. 'I have to get through this programme, Rachel. Don't you have some designs to work on or some emails to answer or whatever it is fashion designers do?'

'Who broke it off? You or her?' Rachel persisted.

His eyes flashed as they met hers. 'If you don't get out I swear to God I will change the terms of our deal right here and now.'

'You know I can't pay you anything substantial until the label is successfully launched,' she said.

'I wasn't talking about the money,' he said, with a dark meaningful look in his eyes.

Rachel's skin began to tingle and her mouth went completely dry. The silence hummed with tension, a throbbing tension that threatened to snap at any second. She ran her tongue out over her lips, tasting where he had been so recently. It was so intimate, so raw and primal to taste the essence of him: minty and fresh and yet unmistakably, dangerously male. What would it feel like to taste his skin, down his sternum, over his flat abdomen and lower? What would it feel like to taste his aroused flesh, to slide her tongue over the engorged length of him, to tease her tastebuds with the musk of his maleness?

'Rachel.'

'Y-yes?' She almost gulped the word as she met his gaze. Could he see where her mind had been straying? Could he sense how attracted she was to him? She wanted to hide it. How could she want a man who had revenge as his motive for having her here with him like this? How could she possibly want to feel his mouth on hers again? How could she possibly feel as if her life would be over if he didn't want her the way she wanted him?

'Leave,' he said somewhat heavily. 'I have work to do.'

Her gaze went to the chair that was too far away for him to reach. 'I could help you if you like,' she offered, stepping forward to bring the chair closer.

'Damn it to hell, I told you to leave,' he bit the words out. 'Just get the hell out of here, do you hear me?'

Rachel's hands fell off the back of the wheelchair, her heart slipping sideways in her chest. 'I'm sorry…' Her voice came out soft and uncertain. 'I was only trying to help…'

'I don't need your help,' he threw back with a searing glare. 'I can do this. I *will* do this. I don't need you or anyone to help me.'

Rachel left the gym and gently closed the door behind her. She blew out a shaky breath, not sure she was going to be able to handle such a strong and fiercely proud man. But this time his anger and bitterness were directed more at himself than at her, she thought. He hated being vulnerable. He hated having to rely on others to do the tasks he normally took for granted. His plans for her to act as his mistress showed how keen he was to show the world nothing had changed. She wasn't happy with being part of his plan but she couldn't see a way out of it. She would have to say yes and live with the consequences.

Alessandro let out a long ragged breath once Rachel had left. She had caught him at his most vulnerable and it made him hate her for it. His muscles ached and burned but not half as much as he ached and burned to possess her. Kissing her had been a crazy move on his part. He had felt those unbelievably soft lips respond to his and within seconds he had felt his steely control slipping. She had the sensual power to humiliate him like no other woman. Had she enjoyed watching him struggle to regain his mobility? Was that why she had refused to leave—so she could document every agonising step of his journey back to wholeness? How could he trust her when she had acted so unpredictably in the past? He had not seen her rejection coming. That was what tortured him the most. He had been so utterly beguiled by her that he hadn't seen the game she had been playing.

He gripped the equipment with hands that shook with determination. He was not going to let her do it again. He would lock away his feelings and deal with her on a physical level only. That way when the time was up he would be able to get the closure he had so longed for.

Rachel sat and looked out of the window later that day, chewing on the end of her pencil as she took in the glorious view of the gardens. There was a wisteria climbing rampantly over an arbour, and even though the pendulous blooms of spring had mostly fallen there were still one or two, the scent so strong she could smell it through the open window. It was such an inspiring place to be, far better than any hotel she had envisaged staying in. Already she had drawn several designs for gowns that reflected the old-world glamour of the villa. She could imagine soirées here in the past, people spilling out into the colourful and fragrant garden, the champagne flowing, a string quartet playing, perhaps a few couples dancing. It was such a romantic setting, perfect for falling in love...

She dropped the pencil onto the little desk and sat up straight in her chair. There was no way she was going to fall in love, not with Alessandro. He seemed incapable of the depth of emotion it took for a relationship to survive. His feelings were private, off limits, not to be examined. Had she been the one to do that to him? Had her immaturity and selfishness shut him down for good? If so, what could she do to repair the damage she had caused?

CHAPTER SIX

RACHEL was putting the finishing touches to the table in the formal dining room when she heard the sound of the lift being activated. She felt her breath stall momentarily and her skin tingle with alertness.

She stepped back from the table, smoothing her hair back with a hand that wasn't quite steady. She had dressed in one of her own designs, a long silver gown that had hundreds of hand-stitched Swarovski crystals over the bodice. She wasn't sure why she had gone to so much trouble. The occasion hardly called for it, but the magnificence of the villa and its atmosphere made her feel as if every dinner here should be an important event.

Alessandro appeared at the doorway, not in his wheelchair this time, but leaning on a pair of crutches.

'You're walking!' Rachel said in surprise.

'You could call it that,' he said with a wry look.

'I think it's wonderful,' she said. 'All your hard work is starting to pay off.'

'Yes.' He was silent for a moment as his gaze took in her appearance. 'You look very beautiful this evening,' he said.

She felt her cheeks glow from his compliment and lowered her gaze. 'Thank you.'

'But I wonder if I should eat what you have prepared for me,' he added.

Rachel looked at him in confusion. 'Why do you say that?'

He gave her a look that was rueful. 'I was rather brusque with you earlier today. I thought perhaps as a consequence of my behaviour I should be concerned about you lacing my food with something poisonous.'

Rachel held his gaze. 'The only thing I have on hand to poison you with is my tongue.'

He smiled in amusement, the action completely transforming his features. Rachel felt a kick in her belly, a jerky reminder that she was in no way immune to him when he chose to lay on the charm.

'Then I will have to stay well away from your tongue, won't I?' he said with a glint in his eye.

She held that look for as long as she dared. 'Yes, you will,' she said but her voice came out husky and soft, nothing like she had intended.

He shifted his gaze and brought himself closer to the table using the crutches. It was clearly an effort for him but she stood back, reluctant to offer help in case he was annoyed or misread it as pity.

'Thank you,' he said once he was seated at the table.

'For what?' Rachel asked.

'For not treating me like an invalid.'

'But you're not an invalid,' she said. 'You've already made amazing progress in the short time I've been here. I don't think it will be long before you're totally recovered.'

There was a little silence.

'How did you do it last night?' Rachel asked.

'How did I do what?'

'How did you get to the table without assistance?' she asked. 'I didn't see your chair anywhere or the crutches.'

'I can walk short distances by using the furniture as a support,' he said. 'I left the chair out of sight until you had gone upstairs.'

'Why did you leave it until last night to reveal your condition?'

He studied her for a long moment. 'I wanted to make sure you were committed to staying here for the money, not out of pity.'

Rachel frowned at him. 'You'd prefer me to be here just for the money instead of out of compassion?'

'I knew I could count on your desire for money.'

She took her seat, a frown still pulling at her brow. His opinion of her was appalling but no more than she deserved given her treatment of him in the past. How could she redeem herself? She needed the money. She couldn't walk away from the deal even if she wanted to for her pride's sake.

He looked at her with an inscrutable expression. 'That dress you're wearing. Is it one of your own designs?'

Rachel slid her hands down the sides of her dress. 'This old thing?' she quipped. 'It's just something I whipped up one afternoon when I had nothing better to do.'

'So you sew as well as design?' he asked.

'Yes, of course. It's how I got started. I played around with making my own stuff and then I found people would stop me in the street or at a function I was attending and ask me where I got my dress. I decided I had something to offer so I went to design school. That's where I met my friend Caitlyn. We decided to join forces. But I feel I've let her down…' She bit her lip. 'She invested a lot of money in getting us up and running, much more than I did. I was left a little short…well,

I won't bore you with the details but things were not looking that good for me after I ended things with Craig. There wasn't a lending institution that would even give me an interview, let alone a loan.'

He sat looking at her, still with that unreadable expression cloaking his thoughts and feelings.

The silence went on and on and on.

Rachel shifted her weight and waved a hand in the direction of the kitchen. 'I guess I should serve up the first course…'

'So what have you decided?' he asked.

She glanced at the document he had set by his place setting. 'I think you already know I have no choice but to accept your conditions,' she said.

'Think of it this way,' he said, handing her the papers and a pen. 'Your relationship with me will be the shortest of any I have had so far, less than a month.'

Rachel pursed her lips and looked through the document. It was much the same as the previous one. She had to sign a confidentiality clause and she would receive nothing other than the backing of her label and a generous allowance for every day she spent with him. After their relationship was terminated all business to do with the label would be conducted through one of his management team. It felt so cold and calculated. She hated signing her name to such a contract but the faces of her staff and Caitlyn swam before her eyes, and so she scribbled her name with a deep sigh of resignation.

'I will pour the wine,' Alessandro said, putting the papers aside to reach for the bottle Rachel had already set out.

When she came back with their starters the wine glasses were full and the tense atmosphere had eased. She sat down opposite Alessandro and did her best to pretend this was just like any other dinner between two people who had chosen to spend some time together.

'This is a lovely place you have here, Alessandro,' she said. 'I find it so inspiring. I worked on heaps of designs this afternoon just by looking out at the gardens.'

'I am glad you like it,' he said. 'So tell me about the designs you've been working on. What in particular inspired you?'

She drew in a breath and then released it as she picked up her wine glass, cupping it with both hands as she gathered her thoughts. 'I don't know…just the whole atmosphere here, I guess. I don't know the history of the place but it seems the sort of villa that in the past has been at the heart of society: parties, gatherings, celebrations—that sort of thing. I can picture in my mind the women dressed in gorgeous gowns, the men in tuxedos. The gardens are spectacular. I can smell the flowers from my bedroom. It would be a great venue for a wedding…' She stopped and lowered her gaze, dipping her head to her glass and taking a sip of her wine. What on earth was she talking about weddings for?

'Have you ever designed a wedding gown?' Alessandro asked.

Rachel put her glass down and met his gaze. 'Yes, a couple by request and it was a great experience. It's something Caitlyn and I have considered branching further into but it all depends on finances.'

'Do you miss your modelling career?' Alessandro asked after another short silence.

'Yes and no,' Rachel admitted. 'I found some aspects of it wonderful. I loved all the wonderful clothes and the buzz of a show, but there was always a downside. The constant battle to be what the latest trend demanded, the competition between girls you thought were your friends but weren't. I found it hard to work out what was real and what was false. I like the other side of the catwalk. I can do my thing without the other stuff.'

'I guess the advantage you have now is you know how both sides work,' he said. 'You can work the system, so to speak.'

'Is that what you do?' Rachel asked. 'It's a rags-to-riches tale most people from your background only ever dream of.'

'I had some luck but most of it was hard work,' he said. 'I didn't want to waste any opportunity that came along. I worked hard, got to understand things from the ground up, and then made the most of the opportunities that arose. I am no different from any other self-made businessman. You don't have to be born to wealth to be successful.'

She picked up her glass for something to do with her hands. 'I've always wanted to explain about that night…the night of my engagement…'

'Forget about it,' Alessandro said. 'Even if you had felt something for me your father would have forbidden any connection between us. He would have cut you off without a penny.'

'If I had loved you I wouldn't have let my father's opinions matter one little bit,' she said. 'Love is worth much more than any amount of money.'

Alessandro curled his lip in a mocking manner. 'So in spite of your broken engagement your head is still full of romantic notions about true love, is it?'

'I believe in love,' she said. 'I believe it's possible to find fulfilment in a relationship with someone. I think it takes work but I still believe it's possible to have a long and happy life with a partner, growing and changing together rather than drifting apart.'

'So you intend to marry and have children one day?' he asked.

Rachel toyed again with the rim of her glass. 'I would like to think that is going to be a part of my future,' she said. 'I can't see the point in working hard for years on end with no one to share it with. Life is all about connecting with others. It's too lonely otherwise.'

A small silence ensued as Alessandro topped up their glasses.

'What about you?' Rachel asked. 'Do you see yourself settling down one day with a wife and family?'

He put the wine bottle back in its cooler before he answered. 'I have no immediate plans to do so.' He gave a small rueful twist of his mouth. 'I find relationships hard work. I am not good at long-term commitment. No doubt it comes from my background, the lack of good modelling or a strong sense of family or something. The longest relationship I have had was six weeks. The last two of them were some of the most miserable days of my life and hers too, I would imagine. We didn't part as friends.'

'Did you love her?'

'No.'

'Did she love you?'

'She loved the lifestyle I could give her,' he said. 'Most if not all women I have met do. But no amount of luxury holidays and gifts of expensive jewellery can make up for not being connected on the levels that count.'

'I don't agree that most women fall in love with a rich man's lifestyle,' Rachel said. 'You make us all sound like a bunch of greedy, shallow gold-diggers who don't care about anything but their hair and clothes and how many carats are in the diamonds in their ears or around their necks. I think you've been hanging around the wrong women way too long. You need to get out more, to mix in other circles for a change.'

He gave her an indolent smile. 'Maybe before you leave you could set me up with someone you think would be suitable. Someone who could make me change my mind. Do you have anyone in mind?'

Rachel felt that funny little fluttery pulse between her thighs again. Every time he looked at her a certain way she felt another piece of her armour slip away. He was so attractive when he was in a teasing mood. He was attractive in just about any mood, which was even more alarming to her. She found his brooding looks just as mesmerising as his playful ones. And she still hadn't been able to forget about that kiss in the gym. Nor had she forgotten the feel of his hard body pressing down on hers, the way it had made her feel, the ache and longing that were still burning deep inside her. 'I am sure you are quite capable of finding a partner all by yourself,' she said with a touch of asperity. 'I have no qualifications as a matchmaker. I haven't exactly had the best of luck myself in the relationships area.'

'Perhaps we are two of a kind, Rachel,' he said, still with that lazy half-smile. 'Two people who are unlucky in love.' He picked up his glass and touched it against hers. 'Let us drink a toast. To finding what we both want.'

Rachel sipped her wine, wondering what exactly it was that Alessandro wanted. He had said sleeping with him was optional but she could feel the undercurrent of sexual tension in the air when they were together. A simmering tension that seemed to build as each minute passed. She could feel it now, especially when he looked at her with those intensely dark blue eyes. She felt as if she were being cast under a spell. The more time she spent with him, the more she felt her defences crumbling. He might have been the one in lust with her in the past, but this time around she was being drawn to him in a way she could neither explain nor control. She had never thought of herself as a particularly sensual person and her experience with Craig had only reinforced that. His criticisms of her had cut her deeply, making her feel unlovable and unattractive. Sex had been a physical act that hadn't touched her at all emotionally. But Alessandro challenged all of her assumptions about herself. With him she felt alive sensually. With him she felt desire hot and strong. With him she felt a need that would not go away.

But it would *have* to go away if she was to come out of this arrangement with her emotions intact. He wasn't interested in anything other than a temporary dalliance. He had signed her up for a limited time and she would do well to remember it. This was a contract relationship, a business transaction that had no emotional bearing whatsoever. She would be a fool to fall in love with him now. It was too late. The chance for love had been five years ago. Why hadn't she realised it at the time? She looked at him across the table and felt her heart tighten painfully. She had missed her chance with him. There was no going back.

It was too late.

'Is everything all right?' Alessandro asked.

Rachel gave him a rueful look. 'I was just thinking about how different things would have been if I'd had more time with you back then.'

His gaze steadied on hers, holding it for a beat or two. 'We weren't exactly strangers, Rachel. I'd been working for your father for three years.'

'I know, but I was only starting to get to know you when we started dating,' she said. 'I think I was only starting to get to know myself...'

His smile was fleeting. 'You were young and used to living a certain way. It would never have worked between us.'

Rachel wondered if that were true. Did a difference in background really matter? Even royalty married commoners these days and lived happily together. Alessandro had qualities she had never seen in any other man. She suspected his difficult upbringing had given him a depth of wisdom that someone from a privileged background could never possess.

The meal progressed until it was time to clear away. Rachel pushed back from the table but Alessandro's hand came down on hers and held her fast. Her eyes met his, heat pooling in her belly when she saw the dark blue flame of his gaze. 'Thank you for doing dinner,' he said. 'I am sorry I can't be of much help in clearing away.'

Rachel felt the burn of his touch, making every pore of her skin tingle. 'That's OK,' she said huskily. 'I'll make coffee and bring it into the salon, shall I?'

He slowly released her hand. 'That would be perfect,' he said. 'I will meet you in there in a few minutes. I have a call to make.'

When Rachel came into the salon a short time later Alessandro was sitting in one of the leather sofas, his long legs stretched out in front of him. The crutches were against the wall close by. He put his mobile phone away and moved his legs as she put the coffee on the table in front of him.

He patted the seat beside him. 'Come,' he said. 'Don't hover over there as if you are afraid I am going to bite you.'

Rachel came over and sat down beside him, careful not

to allow her thighs to get too close to his. But even so she felt the warmth of his body, and the citrus spice of his aftershave made her long to lean closer to breathe more of its intoxicating and alluring scent. It had been a mistake to sit beside him. She knew it as soon as he turned his head to look at her. There was no way she could disguise her reaction to him. Her breathing was all over the place, her heart rate rising as every pulsing second passed.

He put a finger to her temple where a strand of her hair had fallen across, his touch so light and tender as he brushed it back from her forehead it made her breath hitch in her throat. 'Like silk,' he said, picking up another tiny strand and running it through his fingers. 'Your hair is like spun silk.'

'It's too fine and I can never control it,' she said. 'Sometimes I think I should just cut it all off.'

He cupped the back of her head, his fingers setting every sensory nerve on her scalp alight. 'No, don't do that,' he said, his eyes locking on hers, dark, intense, serious.

Rachel sent the tip of her tongue out over her lips, a nervous, anticipatory gesture she couldn't quite control in time. She watched as his eyes moved to her mouth, and the way his tongue did the very same thing over the much drier landscape of his lips, leaving a faint glisten of moisture that instantly disappeared. She brought her hand up, her index finger tracing the line of his mouth in intimate detail, the smooth skin of her fingertip catching on the dry lines of his lips. 'You should use lip balm when you go to bed at night,' she said in a voice that was so soft it was close to a whisper.

His eyes were even darker now as they came back to hers. 'Is that what you do to keep your lips so soft?' he asked, placing the pad of his broad thumb on the pillow of her bottom lip, moving it back and forth in a slow caress that sent the sensitive nerves into a frenzy.

'I—I sometimes forget…' she said, swallowing as his mouth inched closer.

'I guess it becomes a habit if you do it often enough,' he said just above her lips, his voice low and deep and raspy.

'Yes…it just becomes part of your nightly routine,' she said, mesmerised by his mouth so close now she could feel his warm breath on her lips.

'Like flossing and brushing your teeth,' he said, caressing her top lip this time, taking his time over the bee-sting curve.

'Yes…' She could barely take in a breath; her chest felt so tight, her heart hammering now.

His hands cupped her face, his thumbs either side of her mouth, touching the sensitive corners. 'I've been doing some thinking. If we are to convince others of the authenticity of our relationship we should really practise our moves a little more.'

Rachel's heart gave a tumble. 'Moves?'

'Yes,' he said. 'Like kissing, touching, all the things lovers do in public.'

Her forehead crinkled slightly. 'But I thought—'

He silenced her with both of his thumbs pressing softly against her lips. 'Don't think, *cara*,' he said. 'Just feel what is there between us. Feel the chemistry. Feel the electricity. Feel the heat.'

Rachel could feel the heat all right. She could feel it through the pads of his thumbs on her lips. She could feel it in her breasts, the tingles of her skin making her ache for him to touch her there. She felt it in her lower body, the feminine heart of her contracting with a pulse of longing that was activated just by him looking at her. It was magnified a thousandfold with his touch. She moved her lips against the soft pressure of his touch, her tongue pushing through to make contact. She saw the flare of his pupils and heard the intake of his breath as he moved his thumbs aside and brought his head down and sealed her mouth with his.

It was an erotic, heart-stopping kiss. It brought her senses alive in a way she had never imagined possible. She felt every movement of his mouth on hers, every subtle turn, every slide or glide, every dart and thrust of his tongue as he took the kiss to a deeper, far more intimate level. Her insides melted as he pushed her further back on the leather sofa, his weight coming over her, his chest crushing her breasts, making her aware of her tightly erect nipples and how they longed for more of his touch. She felt the stirring of his erection against her feminine mound, the temptation of having him inside her, the feeling of the friction of his body against hers totally and utterly overwhelming. She pushed up against him with her pelvis, aching for more contact, her need for him so desperate she made soft little whimpering sounds that came from deep inside her. It was as if a longing had been unleashed, an inner yearning she had never even realised she possessed until now.

He pushed down against her, the primal grinding of his male body against hers reminding her of everything that was different about them: his maleness, her femaleness, his hardness, her softness. The pounding of his blood as he rocked in time with her delighted her, making her realise just how much she had underestimated the chemistry that had always existed between them. It burned like a fire between them. It was a conflagration of the senses. They had only to be in the same room as each other for it to fire off. She felt that fire now. She felt it in every part of her body, especially now as his tongue curled around hers, calling hers into a sexy combat that mimicked what their bodies craved above all else. She felt it in the tautness of his muscles, the knife-edge tension, and the crawling need of the flesh that was like a thirst that could not be denied. She was thirsty. She was parched. She was desperate to be filled with the essence of him, to feel her female world tipped on its axis, to feel the possession of his body as she had never felt before.

'I shouldn't have started this.' Alessandro pulled back from her, his weight supported by his elbows as he looked down at her.

Rachel didn't want to stop. She wanted it to continue. She wanted it all. She wanted to feel him take her to the place she knew existed but had never felt personally. She wanted to feel what it felt like to have two bodies totally in tune with each other, the chemistry just right, the need to be fulfilled overtaking any other caution. She didn't want to think about why she was here and how it had been engineered. She didn't want to think about the fact that he was intent on revenge. All she wanted to think about was how much she wanted him and he wanted her. That was all that counted. It was not something he could deny, no matter how much he said to the contrary. She had felt it. She could still feel it. She felt it in her own body. It was a raging inferno of need that refused to be damped down with a thimbleful of common sense, which was all she possessed right now.

'I want you,' she said, clutching at him. 'I think I've always wanted you.'

He took her hands in one of his and removed them from his chest. 'No, Rachel.'

She frowned at him. 'But you want me. I know you do. You're surely not going to deny it?'

'No. Of course I am not going to deny it.'

'Then…why?'

He moved away from her, spreading the fingers of one hand to comb through his hair. His expression closed over but she could see a tiny nerve pulsing at the side of his mouth as if the control he was harnessing was not quite under his command.

'Alessandro?'

'Leave it, Rachel,' he said.

'Did I do something wrong?' she asked.

He gave her a rueful movement of his lips and then reached out and touched her cheek with his fingertips. 'No, you did nothing wrong.'

Rachel put her hand over his. 'Is it your illness?' she asked softly. 'Are you worried you—?'

His brows snapped together and he pulled his hand out from under hers. 'I said just leave it, Rachel,' he said tightly.

Rachel swallowed. 'I'm sorry.'

He let out a breath, which relaxed his tight expression. 'Don't apologise,' he said. 'You've only been here a couple of days. For now I would like simply to spend time getting to know you as a person. I have just invested a large sum of money into your business. I want to know everything there is to know about you.'

'There's not much to tell,' Rachel said.

'I am sure you are underselling yourself,' Alessandro said. 'For instance, I did not know you could cook. What other talents do you have now that you didn't have before?'

'They're not really talents,' Rachel said. 'More like interests, I guess you would say.'

'Such as?'

'I love wandering around art galleries and museums,' she said. 'I once spent the whole day in The Victoria and Albert Museum in London.'

'When did you visit London?' Alessandro asked.

'A couple of years ago,' she said. 'It was after my father lost everything. I wanted to escape for a while.'

'How long were you abroad?'

'Two months,' Rachel said. 'I went to Paris too. I spent days and days wandering around there. It's such a beautiful city.'

'It can be a very lonely city on your own,' he said. 'It is best to be there with a lover.'

'I am sure you have been there many times with many lovers,' Rachel said.

'I know Paris very well,' he answered with a ghost of a smile. 'I will look forward to sharing it with you next week.'

Rachel tried not to think of all the beautiful women he had escorted all over Europe. She'd bet he had not rejected their advances the way he had hers just now. Her doubts and insecurities haunted her all over again. Craig had berated her so often on how she turned him off. It was hard to know if Alessandro was experiencing the same turn off or whether he was still struggling with the limitations from his illness. Either way she felt ashamed about admitting so openly how much she wanted him. It gave him so much more power over her.

'You didn't think of coming to Italy during that trip?' Alessandro asked.

She looked at his expression but couldn't read it. 'I did think of it. I had heard you had become successful over here. But I didn't think you would want to see me after what I did.'

'So you think I should have forgiven you by now, do you, Rachel?' he asked, still with that unfathomable look on his face.

'I think being bitter doesn't help anyone in the long run,' she said. 'I have many regrets over the past. But I like to think I have put in place steps that will stop me making the same mistakes I did back then.'

His dark eyes held hers for a lengthy moment. 'I guess the next two and a half weeks will prove that one way or the other, will they not?'

'I want to make amends, Alessandro,' she said. 'I really do.'

He didn't answer immediately. She watched as he rose from the sofa and reached for his crutches. 'Goodnight, Rachel,' he said. 'I will see you in the morning.'

Rachel got to her feet, her hands going to a twisted knot in front of her body. He was dismissing her again, showing her he was not the lovesick young man of the past. He was all sophistication and control now. He had kissed her but he had so easily pulled away while her body still hummed and throbbed like a tuning fork struck too hard.

'Goodnight,' she said, her voice coming out soft and husky, but he had already turned and left the room.

CHAPTER SEVEN

WHEN Rachel came downstairs the next morning Lucia was bustling about in the kitchen. She looked up from her task of brewing coffee and smiled. 'Signor Vallini told me you are staying on for the rest of the month,' she said. 'That is very good. It will be good for him to have company. He needs to be distracted from work. He works too hard. No wonder he got sick. I tell him all the time. All work no play makes for a very out-of-balance life.'

'He's certainly very driven,' Rachel said.

'You knew him before, *si*?' Lucia asked.

'Yes, did he tell you?'

Lucia chuckled. 'He didn't need to tell me. I am not blind. I see the sparks that fly.'

'He hates me,' Rachel said with a slump of her shoulders. 'We were dating for a short time five years ago but I ended up engaged to someone else.'

'Ah, now it all makes sense,' Lucia said.

'There isn't a day that's passed that I haven't regretted what I did,' Rachel said. 'I was too young to see what I was throwing away. If we'd had more time together things might have been so different.'

'He will forgive you in time. He is a passionate man. It is the Italian blood in him. He is proud too. Very proud.'

'Is that coffee for him?' Rachel asked, pointing to the tray the housekeeper was setting up.

'Yes,' Lucia said, handing it over the counter. 'He is in the study.'

The door of the study was closed so Rachel had to balance the tray on one bent knee in order to free her hand to knock on it.

'Entrare.'

She entered the room and Alessandro looked up from his computer screen. 'Where's Lucia?' he asked.

'I thought I'd give her a hand,' Rachel said. 'Where would you like this?'

He waved a dismissive hand to a side table near the window overlooking the gardens. 'Leave it over there,' he said, returning his gaze to his computer screen.

Rachel placed the tray where he said and came to stand by his left shoulder. 'What are you working on?' she asked.

He looked at her irritably. 'Don't you have things of your own to do?' he asked.

Rachel stood her ground. 'Why are you being so prickly this morning? Did you get out on the wrong side of the bed or something?'

His dark blue eyes clashed with hers, a tussle of wills, a heated exchange, and the unmistakable sexual tension building with each pulsing second. Almost without realising she was doing it Rachel reached out with her hand, a butterfly touch to the lean shape of his jaw. Her soft skin snagged on the masculine stubble even though he had shaved that morning. She trailed a finger down to his mouth, outlining his lips, top and bottom, all the while feeling her stomach dip and dive as his eyes darkened immeasurably.

'What do you think you are doing?' Alessandro asked in a voice that sounded deep and scratchy.

'I'm not sure...' Her hand fell away as her creamy cheeks bloomed with a soft tide of pink.

Alessandro captured her hand and brought it back to his mouth, his lips moving against the tips of her fingers, watching as her grey-green eyes flared with desire. It pleased him that she wanted him. It was part of the plan: to make her want him and then walk away from her the way she had done to him. Making love with her was something he had dreamed of for years. He dreamed of the silk of her skin moving against his, the movement of her lips, the way she met his tongue with hers, dancing around it until she finally capitulated. Their kiss last night had almost undone him. He wanted to kiss her again. He wanted to touch her and caress her until she remembered only his touch, no one else's. He wanted her like a force that came from somewhere so deep inside him he had no idea how to turn it off. It consumed him. He had lain awake last night burning with need, his body hot and hungry for her and only her. But he was not sure if he could trust his body just yet. What if he couldn't perform as she hinted at last night? That would be the ultimate humiliation and one he wasn't sure she wouldn't use against him once the six months' confidentiality clause was up.

He kept her hand in his, resting it on the top of his thigh, his other arm going around her to bring her closer so she could see the computer screen. 'I am working on a new development in Florence,' he said, 'a refurbishment and overhaul of an old hotel that has been badly managed. It is a big project.'

'It looks it,' she said. 'It looks like a good position.'

'Yes, location is everything, of course.'

He could smell her perfume and the fragrance of her hair.

He could feel the warmth of her hand where it rested on his thigh, burning into his flesh, making his blood pound to fill him. It was exhilarating to feel the nerves come to throbbing life. Maybe his doubts were unwarranted. His body felt as alive as it had ever been, maybe even more so. He clicked on a few more properties for her to see to distract himself from pulling her into his arms. 'This is one I did in Madrid, and this one in Sicily.'

'The decor is wonderful,' she said. 'Do you have a team of interior designers?'

'Yes, I have a lot of very hard-working staff in the corporation,' Alessandro said. 'But I do a lot of the groundwork myself.'

She looked at him again. 'It sounds like you work very hard.'

'It's the only way to get ahead.'

She looked down at her hand resting on his thigh. 'Alessandro…'

He swivelled in the chair so she was in between his thighs, trapped by him. He felt the increasing strength in his muscles. Had her presence here awoken those weakened nerves? For weeks he had struggled with his exercises and yet within a couple of days of having her here his body had come to life in a way he had not thought possible. He burned for her. He ached and burned to possess her, to feel her wrap herself around him, to be his in the most elemental way possible. But while he craved physical closeness with her there was no way he was ever going to allow her close emotionally. He had to keep thinking of her as a gold-digger even if she had changed. It was his armour against her.

'What is it you want, Rachel?' he asked. 'More money? Is that why you are offering yourself to me on a platter? You want to build up your coffers a little bit more now you can see how rich I am?'

Her eyes widened in affront and she tried to pull out of his hold but he kept his thighs firm against hers. 'Why do you always misread my motives?' she said. 'I'm not offering myself, not like that. I thought… I don't know what I thought. Last night when you kissed me…'

'You think you want me,' Alessandro said. 'But it's the money you really want.'

Her face coloured up, hot and angry, the grey in her eyes like lightning flashes in amongst the green. 'You think I would sleep with you just because you're rich and powerful? Is that the type of woman you think I am?'

Alessandro gave her a cynical smile. 'I know exactly the type of woman you are. You are intent on success. If you have to sleep your way to the top you will do it.'

She curled her shapely top lip at him. 'Is that what you did, Alessandro?' she asked. 'Did you sleep with a bunch of rich women to get where you are today? Is that how you did it? Did you prostitute yourself with any old rich hag to—?'

'*Silenzio!*' He pushed himself upright in anger, his barked command ringing in the air.

Rachel took an unsteady step backwards but her hip caught the edge of the desk. She winced in pain and lost her footing. Alessandro reached out to stop her from falling but it meant he had to lift his hands off the desk where he had placed them for balance.

It all seemed to happen so fast and yet each moment was like a freeze frame of a slow-motion film in her brain. She could feel herself going down when Alessandro's strong hands gripped her, but, because he couldn't totally rely on his legs, the weight of him coming down tipped her further off balance.

But rather than land heavily on her, he somehow twisted his body at the last minute and cushioned her fall. She fell on top of him, the air knocked right out of her lungs, her hair hanging over her face, her startled gasp of shock the only sound in the sudden silence.

'Are you all right?' Alessandro asked, his chest rising and falling.

'Y-yes…are you?' Rachel asked, pushing up on her hands to look down at him.

'I'm fine,' he said, taking a deep breath. 'Sorry I couldn't stop you from falling.'

'It wasn't your fault.'

'I forgot about my legs,' he said with a rueful grimace. 'They're getting stronger every day but not strong enough to make such sudden movements.'

'It must be very frustrating for you,' Rachel said, somehow not able to move from where she was lying over him. She felt magnetised to him. She could feel his body below hers, every delicious male inch of him swelling in attraction.

'It is immensely frustrating,' he said, looking at her mouth.

Rachel moistened her lips. She made a move to get up but one of his hands went to her lower back and pressed her down against him. She felt the kicking motion of her heart and the answering echo deep and low in her body when that very same hand glided the entire length of her spine to the nape of her neck. Every sensory nerve went on overdrive, tingles racing across her scalp as his other hand pushed back the curtain of her hair, anchoring it over her left shoulder.

'Stay right there,' he said in a deep, rough around the edges tone.

Rachel felt her insides clench with desire. This was crazy. She was not the sort of girl to succumb to physical lust like this but her body seemed to have other ideas. It was thrumming with a need so strong she felt every nerve in her body quivering with anticipation of sensory release. 'Alessandro, please believe me when I say this is not about the money,' she said. 'It's never been about the money. I've never felt this way before.'

He looked at her for an endless pause, his eyes surveying every nuance of her face. 'I have always dreamed of this moment,' he said.

Rachel managed to croak, 'You have?'

He gave one of his barely there smiles. 'Feeling you like this, your body on mine, feeling the pulse of your blood.'

'You can feel that?' she asked.

He placed a hand against her breast where her heart was pounding. 'I can feel it,' he said. He slowly spread his fingers so they came into contact with her breast; the whole time his gaze was locked on hers, drawing her inexorably into his sensual orbit.

Rachel leaned into the caress, her flesh erupting into flames at the intimate and possessive touch. Her nipple was a tight nub of need, the soft curve of her breast an aching globe that craved the naked glide of his hand and fingers. She wanted him to uncover her, to rip her clothes from her roughly, to devour her with his lips and tongue, but he did neither.

He flipped her over to her back, but gently, as if turning something incredibly precious and fragile. She was now looking up at him, his dark midnight-blue eyes still holding hers in a mesmerising lockdown.

'I have never wanted anyone like I want you,' he said. 'But I need to know this is about mutual attraction, not you feeling you have to sell your body to save your company.'

She looked deeply into his eyes. 'I am grateful, but you have to understand I would never sell myself for any price. I did that before and I have always regretted it. You have no idea how much. But I want you for you. Not because of money, just because I want you. I want to know what it feels like to have you inside me. I want to know what it feels like to be in sync with someone physically. I've never felt that before.'

He frowned as he looked down at her. 'You weren't satisfied with Hughson?'

'I hated sleeping with him,' she said, lowering her eyes. 'It was a chore. He blamed me but I kept thinking of how it felt to kiss you and I always wondered...'

He lifted her chin to keep her gaze locked on his. 'You wondered what?'

'I wondered what it would feel like to be with you,' she said. 'I often wondered if I had slept with you back then if I would have made the same choice.'

He was still frowning darkly. 'So you hadn't slept with him before your engagement?'

'No,' she said. 'We'd kissed as teenagers. I had a massive crush on him for most of my adolescence but I'd never gone that far. I had a mild fling with someone in my final year of school but even that was something I'd rather forget.'

He began stroking her face, a gentle rhythmic motion that was so tender it made her heart swell. 'So if I was to make love to you now it would be like your very first time,' he said.

She smiled up at him ruefully. 'I guess so...'

His eyes held hers for a moment, his expression clouding. 'Rachel, there's a chance the first time between us might not live up to your expectations.'

Rachel felt the all too familiar doubts surround her like unwanted guests. 'I can learn how to be better at it,' she said.

'I know I need to relax, everyone says that about sex, that it's in your mind, not so much your body. You can teach me. I feel safe and comfortable with you. That will help, won't it?'

Alessandro cupped her cheek, his thumb tracing over her bottom lip. 'I wasn't talking about you, *cara*.' He paused for a beat, wondering if he was shooting himself in the foot but doing it anyway. 'It's my performance I am most concerned about.'

She looked at him with tears in her eyes. 'It doesn't matter,' she said. 'Just being with you will be enough. I just want to be held by you.'

Alessandro was not used to feeling his heart contract as if it had been slammed between two bookends. He'd been expecting ridicule but instead had got compassion. It made him wonder if he had misjudged her. Her revelations about her sexual history with Hughson had stunned him. Alessandro had always seen her as a highly sensual young woman. He had felt it every time she had been in his arms. How that brute had destroyed her confidence with his selfish handling of her was unforgivable. She deserved so much better. Even if he couldn't give her everything she wanted at least he could give her back her sexual confidence.

Rachel frowned as he made to get up off the floor. 'What are you doing?' she asked.

He pulled himself upright and held a hand out for her. 'I am not making love to you for the first time on my study floor,' he said. 'I have a little more class than that these days.'

Rachel stood in the circle of his arms. 'I think you've always had class, Alessandro. I just didn't see it the first time.'

He smiled a little ruefully as he reached for his crutch. 'I would like to be able to carry you upstairs to my room but I am not quite able to do that as yet. I'm afraid you will have to walk there all by yourself.'

She brushed his mouth with hers. 'How about I meet you there in a few minutes?'

He kissed her back, lingeringly. 'Don't take too long,' he said, trailing a finger down her cheek.

She held his hand to her face for a moment. 'I won't,' she promised.

Alessandro was in his bedroom when Rachel came in. She had dressed in a silky bathrobe but last minute shyness had made her keep her underwear on. He was still dressed in the clothes he had been wearing earlier and she wondered if he had done that to give her an out in case she had changed her mind. It made her realise how much her feelings towards him had changed. Two days ago she had thought she hated him and yet now she felt as if he was the only man on earth she could ever love.

'I wondered if you might change your mind,' Alessandro said. 'If you have, it's fine.'

'I'm here because I want to be here,' Rachel said. 'No one has forced me.'

'Come here.' He patted the bed beside him.

She walked to where he was sitting, feeling shy and awkward. 'I'm not very good at this,' she said. 'I hope you're not going to be disappointed.'

He took her hand and brought it up to his lips. 'Stop criticising yourself,' he said. 'You're beautiful. Every part of you is beautiful and irresistible to me.'

She looked into his eyes and saw the naked need he had for her. It thrilled her to think he had never stopped wanting her. 'Hold me?' she said softly. 'Please?'

He smiled a slow sensual smile as he brought his mouth to hers in a kiss that began slowly, a gentle assault on her senses that built to a crescendo of mutual need. She kissed him back with all the built up longing of her soul. She craved this connection with him; she craved the fulfilment of the flesh that had been denied her for so long.

It was a magical journey exploring his body as he explored hers. Clothes were removed article by article, skin uncovered, kisses planted softly, then with more pressure as desire burned like a flame. Rachel kissed the strong column of his throat, her soft lips catching on his stubble, an intoxicating reminder of his maleness. She went lower, down his sternum, circling each of his flat nipples with the point of her tongue. She discovered he had a ticklish hip and he laughingly growled and turned her onto her back, leaning over her to subject her to the same journey of discovery.

He kissed the sensitive skin of her neck, lingering over her ear lobes before moving to the fine framework of her collarbones. He moved lower to gently uncover her breasts, removing her bra with worshipful hands, before cupping her softly. 'So beautiful,' he said in a voice gruff with desire.

Rachel's insecurity about her body disappeared under the stroke and glide of his hands. And then when his mouth came over her breast she felt her back arch in absolute delight. His mouth was warm, the gentle scrape of his teeth as he teased her nipple sending her senses into a vortex. He explored her other breast, taking his time, building her need for him so much she could feel her body weeping with moisture in preparation for him. He went from her breasts to her belly button, teasing the tiny cave with his tongue. The nerves that led to her feminine core tensed and pulsated with longing as he went lower, each one screaming out for more of his touch. It was such an intimate act and one she had never felt comfortable with with her ex-fiancé, mainly because he had made her feel so inadequate for not responding the way he wanted. She automatically tensed as she recalled all the horrible insults he had flung at her.

Alessandro cupped her mound gently with his hand, not invading her, just holding her. 'Are you OK with this?' he asked.

Rachel bit on her lip. 'I told you I'm not very good at this...'

He moved up so he could brush her hair back from her face. 'No one is rating your performance, *cara*,' he said. 'It takes time for two lovers to get the moves right. What works for one person doesn't always work for another.'

She looked into his eyes. 'You're so much more experienced than I am...'

'That's not something to be ashamed of,' he said. 'Having sex for the sake of having sex is not the same as making love.'

Rachel touched his lips with her fingers. 'Are we having sex or making love?' she asked.

He kissed the tips of her fingers. 'I think you already know the answer to that,' he said and covered her mouth with his own.

He kissed her long and tenderly, drawing from her a response that made her feel giddy with longing. Her lower body ached with a hollow feeling, a twitchy ache that refused to go away. She shifted restlessly beneath him but still he kissed her, his hands caressing her breasts and stomach but going no lower.

'Please...' she said against his mouth. 'I want you. I want you so much.'

Alessandro parted her with his fingers, his touch sending electric shocks of reaction through her. She leaned into his caress, seeking more, wanting and craving more and more. He stroked her, teasing the engorged heart of her into a pulsating bud of need that was ready to explode. The climactic release hit her like a smashing wave, sensations rolling over her and through her like a tiny shell being tossed about in a tumultuous ocean. She felt the quivers of her flesh as she came back from the summit, tiny aftershocks that rippled through her body, leaving her limbless in his hold. 'Oh, God…' she breathed in wonder. 'Oh, God…'

'It will get better,' Alessandro said.

'You think so?' Rachel asked.

'I know so,' he said and kissed her again.

This time Rachel wanted to touch him, to explore him the way he had her. She took him in her hands, loving the feel of him, the steely length so turgid with need. He was oozing moisture and she realised how long he had been waiting for his own release. She was not used to such patience in a lover. 'Am I doing it right?' she asked as she moved her hand up and down his erection.

'Perfect,' he said breathing heavily. 'But I need to get a condom before we go any further.'

Rachel watched as he leaned across and took a condom from his bedside drawer. She took pleasure in helping him apply it, gaining confidence with every caress. He was careful with his weight as he settled between her legs, kissing her mouth with a growing urgency as his need grew. She loved the feeling of him gliding into her feminine heat. He took his time, not rushing her but waiting until she accepted him before going deeper. It was nothing like her first time as a teenager. It was nothing like anything she had experienced with her ex. This was so far from anything she had ever felt before. Her body was blooming with feeling, each sensation as he moved within her making her feel the pleasure building all over again.

And even then he waited for her to reach that pinnacle before he took his own pleasure. She felt the aftershocks of her earth-shattering orgasm trigger his. He groaned deeply, his body thrusting in those few precious seconds of bliss as he emptied himself. She felt the rise of goose bumps on his back and shoulders and felt satisfied that he had been just as undone as she had. She held him close, reluctant to move away in case the magic spell of fulfilment was broken.

Alessandro felt the light dancing of her fingertips up and down his spine, the caressing movements so natural and uninhibited he was tempted to stay there like that for ever. But then reality checked in with extra baggage. Tying himself to her for any longer than he already had was unthinkable. He had made himself a promise and he would keep it. Their relationship was a business deal. The investment he had made was financial, not emotional, and it would stay that way.

As he moved away Rachel sensed a change in him. He seemed to have closed off again, shutting her out. It was such a stark change from the intimacy they had just shared. She had hoped... She wasn't sure what she had hoped. He didn't love her. He had never loved her. He had told her he had wanted to be with her in the past to climb up in society. But somehow while they had been making love she had felt stirrings inside her that she felt were much more than physical desire. She had secretly hoped he was feeling those same stirrings. 'Alessandro?'

He disposed of the condom before he turned to face her. 'You were wonderful, Rachel,' he said. 'You should have no doubts about your ability to give and receive pleasure. Any man would be delighted to have you as his partner.'

Any man but him, she assumed he meant. She tried to read his expression but there was nothing to suggest he was feeling anything like she was feeling. Disappointment hurtled through her. She was such a romantic fool. Of course he wasn't affected. It was just sex to him. She was just another woman he had bedded, admittedly one he had wanted to bed a long time. He was probably feeling pretty pleased with himself. He had finally got what he wanted. That box was finally ticked. Mission accomplished. 'Glad you enjoyed the experience,' she said and got off the bed and wrapped herself in her bathrobe. 'Would you go as far as giving me a ten out of ten?'

His brows moved together. 'What's that supposed to mean?'

'I think you know what it means,' she shot back. 'We made love but there's no love. It's just a physical itch we had to scratch.'

His frown deepened as he rose from the bed, holding onto the wall for support. 'You're not making sense, Rachel,' he said. 'What's this talk about love?'

Rachel clamped her lips together but it didn't stop them from trembling.

'Talk to me, for God's sake,' he demanded.

She waited for a moment to compose herself. 'Alessandro, I've always wanted to tell you why I did what I did. Why I chose Craig instead of you. I've always wanted to explain.'

Alessandro's expression darkened broodingly. 'I know why you chose him. He had money and I didn't.'

'It was about money but not the way you think,' Rachel said. 'What you said the other day about my father is so true. I have spent most of my life trying to please him. Do you have any idea of how hard it is to be perfect all the time? I tried to be the best daughter I could be. I tried to be the best I could be at school but I never made the grades my father made. The only time I was able to please him was when I agreed to become engaged to Craig. I had this one chance to be the perfect compliant daughter. I couldn't turn it down.'

He didn't speak. He just stood there waiting for her to continue. It didn't make the telling any easier.

Rachel took a breath and released it on a sigh. 'My father came to see me just before you did that night. He told me if I didn't agree to marry Craig he would never speak to me again. I told him you and I had started seeing each other. He told me you were only interested in me to get ahead in life. He was so angry and I was so frightened of being cast adrift by my only living relative I just went along with it. I couldn't see I had any choice. My father would never have agreed to us being together. I was going to lose either way. I chose to keep what little family I had. It was the wrong choice. Sometimes it's better to be alone than have family who don't want the best for you.'

Finally he spoke. 'You could have explained that to me that night. Why didn't you?'

Rachel hugged her arms across her body. 'I was going to but then Craig barged in. Anyway, you told me the other day you had only wanted to marry me because you saw me as a way into society. It seemed to confirm everything my father had said about you.'

Alessandro pushed a hand through his hair. 'I should never have said that to you the other day.'

Rachel looked at him in surprise. 'Are you saying it wasn't true?'

His frown made two lines appear above the bridge of his

nose. 'What is the good of going over all of this now?' he said. 'It's too late to change anything.'

'Did you love me back then?' she asked.

His gaze was steady on hers. 'I thought I did but it didn't last so it can't have been the real thing, if such a thing exists.'

Rachel felt her heart squeeze in disappointment. 'So it was always just lust…'

'I was twenty-seven years old back then, Rachel,' he said. 'I had spent most of my youth on the streets. I didn't know what love felt like because after my father died I sure as hell hadn't had anyone to love or who loved me back. You were out of my league but I wanted you. When you chose Hughson I hated you so much it was like a poison in my body. I wanted to show you what you had missed out on. It drove me. I worked harder than anyone I know to get where I am now.'

'But you're not happy,' she said.

His eyes hardened. 'I sought success not happiness. Some people are lucky enough to have both.'

'I want both,' Rachel said. 'But if it came to a choice I would chose happiness over success.'

'What a pity you didn't think like that five years ago,' he said with an embittered look.

'Do you think our relationship would have worked?' she asked.

'It might have for a time,' he said. 'It's been my experience that most relationships have a use-by date.'

'Don't you think that's because you're not prepared to work harder at making them work?' she asked.

'What are you suggesting, Rachel?' he asked with a mocking look. 'You want to try again? See what happens this time around? Forget it. I told you the terms of the deal. You got your backing. In less than three weeks we're over. You go back to your life and I go back to mine.'

'A relationship is not a business transaction,' Rachel said.

He gave her a look that cut her heart in two. 'This one is, little rich girl, and you'd better not forget it.'

CHAPTER EIGHT

RACHEL didn't see Alessandro for the rest of the day. Lucia told her he was working on an important business project and did not want to be disturbed.

'He told me to remind you about Rocco Gianatto coming this afternoon to see you about fabrics,' Lucia added. 'He should be here any minute. I'll make coffee and bring it in when he arrives.'

'Thank you, Lucia,' Rachel said. 'I'll wait for him in the salon.'

Lucia brought in a smartly dressed man in his forties a short time later. Rachel rose from the sofa and greeted him with an outstretched hand. 'It was very good of you to come here to see me, Signor Gianatto,' she said.

'It is no problem,' Rocco said with a smile. 'When Alessandro called me he told me about his little accident.'

Rachel wasn't sure what she was supposed to say. Alessandro had told her nothing other than he did not want the press to know about his illness. She wondered if this was a test of some sort, to see if she would be indiscreet at the first opportunity that presented itself. 'He is finding it rather frustrating,' she said at last.

'Yes, spraining his ankle would be rather a nuisance but no doubt you are cheering him up,' Rocco said.

Rachel blushed but forced herself to stay focused on the business at hand. 'Here is my portfolio,' she said, opening it before him on her laptop.

'Alessandro must be very impressed with your work to put his money in your business,' Rocco Gianatto said after several moments of perusing her designs. 'He is a very careful investor, but then who is not these days, *si*?'

'I am very fortunate to have his support,' Rachel said.

'Your designs are quite lovely,' Rocco said. 'I am sure you will do very well.'

'Thank you.'

He reached into his briefcase and handed her a thick folder of fabric samples. 'Here are some of my best fabrics,' he said. 'All top-of-the range quality. Have a look through at your leisure. I will leave my contact details and if you have time to visit the factory before you return home I would be very happy to show you around.'

'You're very kind,' she said.

'Not at all,' he said with another charming smile.

Rachel was about to offer Rocco more coffee when Alessandro appeared in the doorway using only a walking stick. Rachel's eyes widened a fraction but Alessandro simply smiled and moved over to where she was standing. He leaned on the stick and placed his other hand around her waist.

'So you have met my lovely young companion,' he said to Rocco.

'Yes, she is quite lovely, Alessandro,' Rocco said. 'Not your usual type at all. Perhaps you will keep her a little longer than the others, *si*?'

Rachel bristled. 'I am not used to men discussing me as if I am not in the room,' she said.

Alessandro pressed a kiss to the top of her head. 'See what

a little firebrand she is, Rocco? Maybe I will keep her a little longer than the others. She is certainly very entertaining. I think I will miss her when she goes back to Australia.'

'If you are not careful I will leave right this minute,' Rachel shot back.

Alessandro gently tapped her on the end of her nose. 'You know you don't mean that.'

I do, I do! Rachel wanted to scream out loud but instead pressed her lips tightly together. Of course she couldn't leave, not without repaying every penny he had given her. He had covered all his bases. He was too street smart to have left himself open to exploitation. He was toying with her, amusing himself while his business associate looked on in amusement. He couldn't have planned a more effective revenge. It made her love for him turn sour. How could she have been so trusting to have opened her heart to him about Craig's treatment of her, only for him to have turned her into a rich man's plaything, a toy to be picked up and put down when his interest faded?

The door had barely closed on Rocco Gianatto's exit when she swung around to glare at Alessandro. 'How dare you treat me like a cheap little trollop you've bought for your entertainment?'

He leaned on his stick but even so he towered over her. 'You're being overly sensitive. You know the terms we laid down. You agreed to act as my mistress in public. That fact that you chose to sleep with me in private is neither here nor there. It is no one's business but our own.'

She ground her teeth together. 'How can you be so cold-blooded about this? Of course it's different. It changes everything.'

'You are making things complicated when they don't need to be,' he said evenly.

'I don't like people thinking I am sleeping with you for money,' she said. 'You have to admit that's what people are going to automatically assume once they hear about you backing my label. It's certainly what Rocco Gianatto assumed and as far as I could tell you were actively encouraging him to think it.'

'Why do you care so much about what people think?' he asked.

'Why do you care so little?' she flashed back.

'You'll have to get used to it, Rachel, because I've released a press statement,' he said. 'By morning everyone will know you're my mistress.'

'I could release my own press statement,' she threw back.

His eyes pinned hers. 'You could but you know what will happen if you do. You read and signed the agreement.'

'I wish I hadn't come to see you,' she said, stalking to the other side of the room. 'You're the last person I should have come to. I should have known it would backfire on me.'

'How has it backfired on you?' he asked. 'Your company is safe. You've got what you want. I could have continued to refuse to help you but I didn't.'

Rachel turned around to face him. 'You don't get it, do you?'

'What am I supposed to get?'

Rachel shook her head at him. 'Never mind. I'm being stupid as usual.'

'You're not stupid, *cara*,' he said. 'I wish you would not denigrate yourself all the time.'

She let out a sound that was half a laugh. 'You're so nice

to me and yet you want me to leave at the end of the month and never see me again.'

'It has to be that way, Rachel,' he said.

'Why does it?' she asked.

'You live in Australia and I live in Italy,' he said. 'There's one obstacle and there are probably dozens more.'

'You won't compromise, will you?' she asked.

'No.'

Rachel gave him a tight little smile. It seemed important now to hide from him how much he had hurt her. Let him think she was after his money instead of his love. It was easier that way. 'I guess it was worth a try,' she said. 'I quite fancy being the wife of a billionaire. Maybe you could give me a few contacts of yours or even set me up on a blind date once you've finished with me.'

A hard look came into his eyes. 'I'll see what I can do,' he said and left without another word.

Rachel let out a heavy sigh. What was the point of winning a battle when the war was already lost?

Alessandro came in for dinner and frowned when he saw the empty seat opposite his. He felt his chest tighten. Surely she wouldn't have called his bluff? She had too much to lose. She wouldn't walk away from such a binding contract. It would be financial suicide. 'Where is Signorina McCulloch?' he asked Lucia.

'She is not feeling well,' Lucia said. 'She's gone to bed.'

'What's wrong with her?' he asked, frowning.

'Female trouble,' Lucia said matter-of-factly.

Alessandro looked at the empty chair again, his heart rate settling back down to normal again. 'See that she gets everything she needs, will you?'

'*Sì, signor,*' Lucia said. 'I have already given her some paracetamol and a hot-water bottle.'

'*Grazie.*'

'*Signor...?*'

'Lucia, I employ you to cook my meals and keep the villa tidy,' Alessandro said stiffly. 'I do not need your advice on my love life.'

Lucia pursed her lips. '*Sì, Signor.*'

Alessandro picked at his food and ignored the wine altogether. Lucia came in with another course but he waved her away. 'I'm not hungry.'

'Do you want coffee?' she asked as she cleared the table.

'No.'

'A cognac?'

'No.'

'Signor?'

'What?' Alessandro snapped.

'I was about to take a cup of tea up to the signorina,' Lucia said.

Alessandro stood up and reached for his stick. 'You go home, Lucia,' he said. 'Have the rest of the night off, tomorrow too, if you like. I can look after Signorina McCulloch.'

Lucia beamed at him. '*Grazie, signor.*'

Rachel was lying in bed when there was a knock at the door. 'Come in, Lucia,' she said.

The door opened and Alessandro appeared carrying a cup of tea with one hand while the other grasped his walking stick. 'I gave Lucia the rest of the night off,' he said.

'Oh...'

'How are you feeling?' he asked.

Rachel felt her cheeks heating. 'I'm fine.'

He handed her the tea. 'Do you want biscuits or toast or anything?'

'No, this is fine,' she said.

There was a beat or two of silence.

'I'm sorry for being such a nuisance,' Rachel said, not looking at him.

'You're not being a nuisance.'

A moment of silence passed.

'Do you often have painful periods?' he asked.

'Not often,' she said. 'I guess it's the stress or the travelling or both.'

He sat on the edge of the bed. 'It must have been a very worrying time for you over the last couple of years,' he said.

'You have no idea,' Rachel said on a sigh. 'I've fought back so many times. It's cost a fortune in legal fees trying to clear my name. Craig fraudulently used my name in several loans he had taken out. I had no choice but to cover them as best I could. I tried to get another business loan but no one would come near me after that. That's why Caitlyn put in so much of her own money. We've both worked so hard and the thought of losing it all was so terrifying. This trip to Italy was my last hope.'

'But you're OK now,' he said. 'That's the main thing.'

'Yes, thanks to you.' She looked up at him. 'I can't tell you how grateful I am. I'm sorry I was snarly with you earlier. I can be such a cow sometimes.'

He smiled and reached for her hand, squeezing it gently. 'You're forgiven.'

Rachel curled her fingers around his. 'You're doing so well with your walking now,' she said. 'I can't believe the difference in a few days.'

'Perhaps it's been your presence here,' he said with another smile. 'You've been an added incentive.'

She traced the back of his hand with her fingertip. 'It must have been a terrible shock to become so suddenly vulnerable,' she said. 'You've always been so active and strong.'

'Yes, we all to some degree take good health for granted until we are faced with a crisis,' he said. 'It's been a lesson to me. I won't be taking too much for granted again.'

'Lucia says you work too hard, that you need more balance in your life.'

Alessandro frowned. 'Lucia forgets her place sometimes.'

'She cares about you,' Rachel said. 'She wants to see you happy.'

He began to rise from the bed. 'I should let you sleep.'

Rachel reached for his hand to stop him. 'Don't go.'

'Rachel, it's best I go so you can get some rest.'

'I just want someone to hold me,' she said. 'No one has ever done that before. Just hold me. Please?'

Alessandro sat back down and stroked the hair back from her face. 'You haven't drunk your tea.'

'I don't want it,' she said. 'I just want you.'

He lay down beside her and gathered her close. 'I'll leave once you're asleep.'

'Don't leave me,' she said, burrowing closer.

I have to leave, Alessandro thought. *I always leave.*

But when morning came he was still there with his arms around her, the soft breeze of her breath tickling his neck where she was pressed so close to him. She had looked so vulnerable with her beautiful face all washed out and pinched with pain that he hadn't been able to maintain his distance. But now was another story. He had to refocus, to remain strong.

He gently untangled himself from her arms and got off the bed, reaching for his stick for balance. But in spite of his determination he couldn't stop himself from looking down at her for a few more precious moments. She looked so young and innocent in sleep. He thought of waking beside her every morning, not just for a week or two but for the rest of their lives. Was this what his father had felt for his mother? He didn't want to feel anything like that for anyone. It had destroyed his father and it would destroy him. Love was an addiction that could not always be controlled. He had felt it before and it had blinded him. It was better this way, to have his fill of her and let her go, better for both of them. She thought herself in love with him but women were wired that way to associate good sex with emotion. She would move on and find someone else, someone who wanted the same things in life, marriage, commitment, a child or two. He pushed aside the image that came to mind of her swollen with someone else's child. That was taking self-torture way too far.

He bent down and brushed a soft kiss against the plump curve of her mouth. She murmured something but he couldn't quite catch it. She nestled into the pillow and let out a tiny sigh.

He grasped his stick and limped out of the room, closing the door softly behind him.

When Rachel came downstairs Alessandro was out on the terrace. He turned when she came through the French doors and smiled at her. 'You are looking a little less peaky than last night,' he said.

'I'm feeling much better now.'

'I thought if you felt up to it we might go out for breakfast,' he said. 'I gave Lucia the day off and I have to warn you I am no cook.'

'I can make us something,' Rachel offered.

'No, it's probably time we faced the music, so to speak,' he said, nodding towards the paper that was on the table of the outdoor setting.

She couldn't read the article but there was a photo of her that had been sourced from somewhere. She recognised Alessandro's name and hers. She could just imagine what had been said about her. She was glad she couldn't read it. She knew none of it would be flattering. It never was. She would be tagged as one of Alessandro's gold-digging lovers, intent on money and prestige.

'The press will probably be about,' he said. 'They always want an exclusive. Just do your best to ignore them. You don't have to say anything. It's better if you don't.'

'I don't want to go out,' she said. 'I'd rather stay here.'

'Rachel, we have to go out in public sooner or later,' he said. 'This can be a practice run for next week in Paris. It's not a big deal.'

'It's a big deal to me,' she said. 'I don't like being seen as a rich man's mistress. It's demeaning.'

He rolled his eyes in frustration. 'Do you know there are times when I just don't get you? Yesterday you were asking me for contacts so you could land yourself a rich husband. Now you're balking at being seen in public with me. Or is it this stick that is worrying you? Is that what this is about?'

'How can you think that of me?' she gasped. 'How *can* you?'

'I am trying to do the right thing by you, Rachel,' he said. 'Now I am asking you to do something for me. The business meeting in Paris is very important to me. It's a big one, a massive one. I don't want any hint of my illness compromising it. Being seen in public with you both here and there will help my cause. This is your turn to do me a favour. I don't see why you are so hesitant about this. It's not as if it's going to cost you anything.'

'Why is everything always about business with you?' she asked.

'Because that is what counts,' he said. 'I can rely on facts and figures.'

She frowned at him. 'And you can't rely on people?'

'I have taught myself never to rely on people,' he said. 'It doesn't matter who they are, they always let you down in the end.'

'You don't give anyone a chance to prove you wrong about that,' Rachel said. 'You cut people out of your life before you get attached to them.'

He scowled at her. 'When did you become such an expert on relationships?'

Rachel lowered her gaze, stung by his cutting remark. 'I never said I was an expert...'

He tipped up her chin and let out a heavy sigh. 'I'm sorry,' he said. 'That was low of me.'

She tried to smile but her lips wouldn't cooperate. 'It's OK. I know I'm not great at relationships. I guess it's because I'm scared no one will love me unless I do everything that's expected of me. I just wish...I just wish for once in my life I could be loved for just being me.'

He continued to hold her gaze for a pulsing moment before his fingers fell away from propping up her chin. 'Come on,' he said gruffly. 'I want to get this over with.'

The café Alessandro took her to for breakfast overlooked the sparkling blue of the ocean, with the Isle of Capri a jewel in the distance. Rachel had mentally prepared herself for the barrage of the press as soon as they stepped out of the car. She avoided most of the questions by letting Alessandro do the talking. He was polite but firm with them, answering what he wanted to answer and ignoring what he did not.

'Signor Vallini, tell us about your accident.'

'I tripped down some steps,' he said with a self-deprecating smile. 'I was lucky not to have broken both of my ankles.'

'Is it true you are in the process of negotiating a deal with Sheikh Almeed Khaled from Dubai?'

'No comment.'

'How long do you plan to stay in Positano?' another asked.

'Until September,' Alessandro answered.

'Signor Vallini, is it true that you were involved with Miss McCulloch five years ago?' a female journalist pressed forward to ask just as they were about to enter the café.

'Yes, that is true,' he said.

'That's a first, isn't it, Signor Vallini?' the journalist persisted. 'You've never revisited a previous relationship before. Does that mean that we can expect to hear wedding bells in the very near future?'

'No, it just means that Miss McCulloch and I are enjoying spending some time together for the time being,' he said with a frown.

'Miss McCulloch.' The journalist swung to Rachel. 'If Signor Vallini were to ask you to marry him what would you say?'

Rachel smiled back even though it hurt to do so. 'I would say yes.'

She felt Alessandro's hand tighten on hers. 'If you will excuse us?' he said curtly and escorted her into the café.

Once they were seated and coffees were ordered Alessandro

looked at her with brooding intensity. 'You think you can manipulate me into offering you marriage?' he asked in a sharp undertone.

Rachel returned his look. 'I am doing no such thing.'

He frowned. 'Then why say such a ridiculous thing to the press?'

'Because you told me to act like a devoted lover,' she said. 'If I was truly in love with you then of course I would want you to ask me to marry you.'

He continued to frown at her. 'You were supposed to leave all the talking to me.'

'I don't like other people speaking for me,' she threw back.

The waiter came with their coffees and Alessandro sat back. He leaned forward once the waiter had gone, his voice still tight with tension. 'I know what you're up to, Rachel. You want it all: the rich husband, the lifestyle you were brought up with and the security of knowing it can't be taken away from you a second time. But I am not playing ball.'

'I'm not asking you to,' she said. 'I just want the money for my label.'

Alessandro set his jaw as he fought his knee-jerk reaction to her little game with the press. 'I thought we were starting to trust each other but now I'm not so sure you're being straight with me.'

She flicked her hair back from her shoulders. 'You don't trust anyone. That's not my problem, that's yours.'

'Two and a half weeks,' he said through gritted teeth. 'That's all.'

Rachel tossed her head. 'I'll be on that plane so fast you won't get time to say goodbye to me.'

He made a sound in his throat as he reached for his coffee. 'I was a fool to allow you inside the villa.'

'Oh, come on,' Rachel said with a roll of her eyes. 'You laid a trap for me.'

He looked up at her, a frown still pulling at his brow. 'You really think it was me who sabotaged your attempt at finance?'

She arched her brow at him. 'Wasn't it?'

He took a breath and slowly released it. 'Now who's talking about a lack of trust?' he asked.

'But this whole set-up…' Rachel waved a hand to encompass them both. 'You mean you didn't plan it? None of it?'

Alessandro shook his head. 'You turned up at a very inconvenient time for me, Rachel. I wasn't prepared for visitors. There was no way I was going to agree to see you. But then you worked your charm on Lucia. And then, when I got the invitation for the dinner with Sheikh Almeed Khaled I decided there was a way that things could work for both of us.'

Rachel absorbed this new angle on things for a moment or two. She had always thought Alessandro had engineered things to have her under his command, but now it seemed he had simply used the opportunity that she had put in his hands by turning up on his doorstep. 'Tell me about this business thing with the sheikh,' she said. 'Why is it so important?'

'If he chooses my business analysis service it will be the biggest coup of my career,' Alessandro said. 'His inviting me to spend a week in Paris for dinners and meetings is a sign he is coming close to making his decision.'

'And he asked you to bring your current mistress?' Rachel asked.

'Sheikh Almeed Khaled is a bit of a playboy himself,' he said. 'He admires beautiful women. He is rarely without one by his side. But I think in this instance he wants a glimpse into my private life. You will have to be on your best behaviour. I don't want any slip-ups. Just keep in mind how much money you will have to pay back if you don't behave yourself.'

Rachel gave him a little glowering look. 'Do you have to keep reminding me?'

He signalled for the bill. 'Just keep playing by the rules, Rachel,' he said. 'That's all you have to do.'

CHAPTER NINE

THE boutique hotel in Paris was booked out by the sheikh and his entourage and select guests. Security were posted everywhere, their silent uniformed and armed figures making Rachel feel as if she had stepped into another realm, even beyond the privileged one she had grown up in. This was a world of private jets and servants to see to every need. It made her realise again how much Alessandro had achieved. He mixed with the big time movers and shakers as if it was an everyday thing for him.

The last few days at the villa however, had shown her many different sides to his personality. He was a quiet man who liked his own space. He didn't enjoy idle chatter. He was well read and kept himself informed on everything that was going on in the world. He wasn't bombastically opinionated but he had strong, well-thought-out views. He had a sense of humour but it was dry and he didn't waste his smiles. He always treated his staff with respect and politeness. When the team of gardeners arrived to do their weekly maintenance at the villa he was out there with them chatting over plants and hedges as if he were one of the gang. It was a painful reminder of how badly her father had treated him in the past.

Alessandro cupped her elbow as they were shown to their suite of rooms. 'Dinner is not until eight this evening,' he said once they were finally alone. 'Would you like to rest for a while or do something physical?'

Rachel caught the gleam in his dark eyes. Although he had kissed her many times since, they had not made love again. Her body had missed him so much it was like a constant ache. Her period had long gone but she had felt hesitant about encouraging him to make love to her. How could she stop herself from falling in love with him when he made her feel so amazing? The physical sensations he had evoked in her had a counterpoint emotionally. 'What did you have in mind?' she asked, trying to disguise how she was feeling.

He came over and tipped up her chin, looking deeply into her eyes. 'What's wrong?' he asked.

'Nothing,' she said, trying to smile.

His thumb brushed over her lip. 'That smile wasn't genuine,' he said. 'What's going on in that beautiful head of yours? You were very quiet on the trip over. Have I done something to upset you?'

Rachel caught her lip in her teeth for a moment. 'Alessandro… I'm not sure I can separate my feelings from sex like you do.'

'What are you saying?' he asked.

She looked into his eyes but they were shuttered. 'I don't want to fall in love with you.'

'Then don't.'

She frowned at him. 'It doesn't work like that. I can't just shut off my feelings.'

He dropped his hand from her face. 'I told you from the outset how this is going to work,' he said. 'No emotional entanglements. When it's over it's over.'

'But what if one of us doesn't want it to be over?' Rachel asked.

He walked over to the bank of windows that overlooked the Seine and the city below. 'It has to be over,' he said flatly.

Rachel felt her heart contract. 'I want more, Alessandro,' she said.

Alessandro swung around and shot her a dark look. 'It's not going to happen, Rachel.'

'I don't believe you're incapable of love,' she said. 'I just don't believe that.'

Alessandro wanted to believe it too, but he wasn't going to risk revealing his doubts and fears. Five years ago he would have given anything to hear her say she was in love with him. But now he felt a river of fear run through him at the thought of committing himself if she were to state her feelings out loud.

He came back over to her and gripped her by the shoulders. 'Why are you doing this now? I have the biggest meeting of my career within a couple of hours and you are talking about things that are of no consequence.'

'They are of consequence to me,' she shot back.

Alessandro muttered a swear word but his fingers softened on her shoulders. 'I want you,' he said. 'I want you so badly I have found the last few days a torture. But that is all I can give of myself. You have to accept that.'

Rachel looked into those dark sapphire eyes and felt another part of her heart fall away. 'I want you too,' she whispered.

He brought his head down and covered her mouth with his, passionately, possessively, even a little angrily, Rachel thought. His tongue demanded entry and she gave it with a soft whimper of delight. His arms wrapped around her, pulling her close, so close she felt the hot, hard stirring of his arousal. It stoked her desire to feel him growing so hard so quickly. Her body tingled with the flood of sensations that coursed through her. His tongue stroked and then stabbed at hers. His teeth captured her lower lip, tugging on it and then releasing it to salve it with the brushstroke of his tongue. It awakened a roaring furnace inside her with each exquisite caress. She nipped back at him playfully, delighting in the way he made a sound at the back of his throat in response. He backed her towards the bed, his hands already at her clothes, pulling at them, tossing them aside as she did the same to his in a frenzied mutual mission to become naked as quickly as possible.

His mouth engulfed her nipple as he pushed her down on the bed, her legs wrapping around his hips to lock him to her. His erection was rock-hard and she was so moist and so ready she arched up instinctively to receive him. He drove through with a guttural groan of pleasure that made her skin pepper all over with goose bumps. Her body gripped him tightly, ripples of pleasure rolling through her as he thrust deeply, as if he was unable to control the heat and fire of his need. He set a frantic pace but Rachel kept up. Her body moved with his, her hands caressing his back and shoulders, her mouth locked back on his. He coaxed her to climax with his fingers, just the right amount of pressure to have her soaring within seconds. She cried out with the magnitude of it, the cascading sensations so powerful, so earth-shattering she felt dizzy with it.

His orgasm was just as mind-blowing. She felt him brace himself for that final plunge, all of his muscles tensing before he finally let go. He shuddered against her, his groan of pleasure swallowed by the heat of her mouth.

Rachel lay within the circle of his arms, her chest still rising and falling in the aftermath. She wanted to stay connected to him. She loved the feeling of him locked with her like this: so intimate, so earthy and raw, the scent of sex filling her senses. She didn't want him to pull away and close off as he had before. She wanted this time together to be as precious to him as it was to her.

'I probably took that a little fast,' Alessandro said against the sensitive skin of her neck.

Rachel danced her fingertips up and down his spine. 'It wasn't too fast. It was perfect.'

He propped himself up on his elbows, looking down at her with an unreadable expression. 'I should have also used a condom,' he said. 'I'm assuming you're on the pill?'

Rachel wasn't game to tell him she had missed a couple of days when her luggage had gone missing. 'Of course,' she said.

He brushed some hair away from her forehead. 'I should let you get up and shower,' he said.

'I'm quite comfortable here,' she said, tracing her fingertip over the contour of his lips.

He anchored her hand with one of his, holding her gaze like a laser beam as he sucked on her finger. Rachel felt a frisson of excitement run through her as his mouth drew on her, the slight rasp of his tongue and the scrape of his teeth stirring a primal urge inside her to do the same to him, but far more intimately.

She gave him a sultry look as she wriggled out from under him, pushing him down on his back with the flat of her palm against his chest. 'Stay,' she said in a commanding tone.

'I'm not going anywhere,' he said with a glinting smile.

Rachel had never felt so empowered before. She felt gloriously feminine and alive to her senses and to his. She held his smouldering look with one of her own as she trailed her fingers down his chest, stopping briefly at his belly button before going lower. His body responded to her touch, his erection hardening with each movement of her hand. She shimmied down his body, giving him a look from beneath her lashes before she surrounded him with her mouth. She heard him suck in a breath, felt him tense his entire abdomen as she worked her magic on him. This was nothing like the times her ex had insisted she service him. This was not smutty or horrible or distasteful. This was not impersonal or exploitative.

This was sacred.

She breathed in the scent of him, drawing on him with increasing pressure until she felt him come apart. She pulled back just in time to see him spill, his expression contorted with bliss as he hit the summit. His essence anointed her hand, just as it had her body only minutes before.

His breathing gradually slowed and he looked at her, reaching out to touch her face in a stroke of his fingers that was so soft it was like the brush of a feather. He didn't say anything. He just studied her features as if he were committing them to memory. She saw his eyes go to her mouth, and then back to her eyes, to her mouth again, her cheeks and her hair and then back to her eyes. His were dark and serious, shadowed.

Rachel touched the spot between his brows where the skin had puckered in a slight frown. 'I've never enjoyed doing that before until now,' she said softly. 'Somehow it felt different with you. Everything feels different with you.'

He caught her hand and kissed her fingertips, holding her gaze with his. 'You are a very sensual woman,' he said. 'But I have always thought that about you.'

'That's not how Craig would describe me,' Rachel said. 'He told me I was frigid. God, I hate that word.'

His frown deepened. 'You need to move on from what happened with Hughson,' he said. 'You need to stop blaming yourself for his shortcomings.'

'I know,' Rachel said. 'I'm trying to. I'm sorry. I shouldn't have mentioned his name. I know it upsets you.'

He paused for a moment before continuing in a gritty tone. 'I hate thinking about you with him. It churns my gut to think of him touching you without respect or consideration.'

Rachel placed her hand on the side of his face in a soft caress. 'You sound jealous,' she said.

His mouth tightened and he pulled her hand away from his face and moved away, turning his back to her as he got off the bed. 'We need to get ready for dinner,' he said. 'You have the first shower. I need to do another read-through of my proposal.'

Rachel watched as he tossed on a bathrobe, tying it around his waist before he reached for his stick. His expression was shut down all except for a tiny movement at the edge of his mouth, an on-off pulse that he couldn't quite control.

She let out a sigh when he left the room to go to the study area of the suite. He had drawn a line between business and pleasure and she had better not forget it.

Rachel was still putting the final touches to her make-up and hair when Alessandro came out of the dressing room dressed in a black dinner suit. She met his eyes in the mirror, saw the way his pupils flared and she felt a frisson of delight rush down her spine. He might not love her but he desired her. She felt the electric energy of it, the power of it making her skin tingle with awareness.

'You look stunning,' he said.

Rachel was glad she had brought this particular black dress

out of her collection. It was ankle-length with a swirly hem, the cut and design highlighting her slim figure. It was strapless but it had a sheer gossamer-like silk stole that she placed around her shoulders. She had put her hair up, pinning it in place with a Swarovski-crystal-encrusted hair clip. 'Thank you,' she said. 'So do you.'

Alessandro took her hand, his expression turning serious. 'Rachel…'

She felt hope flare like a flame in her chest. 'Yes?'

He raised her hand to his mouth and kissed it. 'It doesn't matter.'

'What did you want to say?' she asked.

He waited a beat before saying, 'I want to thank you for being here with me this week.'

'Did I have a choice?' Rachel asked.

A brooding frown pulled at his brow. 'You could have called my bluff. I've been expecting you to any day now. I know I haven't been the easiest person to be around.'

'Neither of us are perfect, Alessandro,' she said.

'No, perhaps not,' he said, still holding her hand.

Rachel turned his wrist over to look at his watch. 'Isn't it time we went downstairs?'

Alessandro tucked her arm through his. 'Let's get down to business,' he said and led her out of the suite.

After introductions were made the sheikh led them through to the table for dinner. Alessandro watched as Rachel talked to the sheikh about her work as a fashion designer and her life back in Australia. She asked polite questions about his life and work too, which clearly delighted the sheikh. The meal progressed with lively banter that was unlike any of the other staid business dinners Alessandro had suffered through in the past.

Just before coffee was being served Rachel excused herself from the table to visit the powder room.

'What an enchanting partner you have, Alessandro,' the sheikh said. 'She is an asset to you. She is clearly in love with you and not in the least interested in your money. It's a rare find for men like us. I wish I could find someone so genuine.'

Alessandro gave him a forced smile. 'Yes, she is rather gorgeous.'

'Will you marry her?' the sheikh asked.

'I haven't made any firm plans,' Alessandro hedged.

'You don't have to take my advice but I would snap her up before someone else does,' the sheikh said. 'What better place than Paris to propose?'

'I'll give it some serious thought,' Alessandro said trying to withstand the urge to shift in his seat. Was it true? Did Rachel truly love him or was she just a great actor? He thought of the intimacy they had shared, how much she had given of herself, how it had made him feel, how it still made him feel. His blood was still singing through his veins in elation. She had worshipped his body as if no one had ever done before. Was that love or lust or plain and simple gratefulness that her business had not gone under?

'Now, about this business proposal,' the sheikh said, interrupting his private reflections. 'Can we meet tomorrow to go through my portfolio? There will be other meetings during the week but I'll try and keep things to a minimum. I'll have my secretary line up some times that suit us both. You'll no doubt want to spend as much time as possible with Rachel while you are here.'

Rachel came back in and both men rose as she resumed

her seat. 'Thank you,' she said to Alessandro as he pushed in her chair.

'I was just saying to Alessandro what a charming young lady you are, Rachel,' the sheikh said. 'I have enjoyed this evening very much. It was a great pleasure meeting you.'

'That is very kind of you,' Rachel said, blushing. 'I have enjoyed meeting you too.'

'Perhaps we can dine together once Alessandro and I finalise our deal,' he said. 'I hope you enjoy your time together in Paris.'

'Thank you,' Rachel said as he rose to take his leave.

Alessandro led her to the lift back to their suite. 'You certainly made an impression on him,' he said. 'I think you just nailed the deal for me.'

'He's seems a very nice man,' she said. 'But I think he hides behind all that wealth.'

Alessandro glanced down at her sharply. 'What makes you say that?'

She gave a little shrug. 'He's very pleasant but I got the feeling he doesn't allow anyone to get too close.'

He looked away from her to stare at the numbers on the lift. 'Having been on both sides I can see how he would do that,' he said tonelessly. 'You never know who your friends are when you have money.'

She looked up at him. 'Doesn't it get lonely way up there at the top?' she asked.

Alessandro frowned heavily and stabbed at the number of their floor even though it was already illuminated. 'No, it doesn't. I am never without company.'

'Company you pay for one way or the other,' she remarked wryly.

He held the door of the lift back with the stiff bar of his arm. 'What is that supposed to mean?'

She sailed past him, leaving behind a waft of her perfume to tease his nostrils. 'Go figure it out,' she said airily as she released her bound hair from its clip.

Alessandro thrust the door of their suite open. 'Damn it, Rachel, what are you playing at now?'

She turned and looked at him, her beautiful face defiant and proud surrounded by that cloud of fragrant hair. 'I'm going to bed. I'm tired of playing the rich man's mistress. I'm now officially off duty.'

Alessandro snagged one of her arms as she began to flounce past. 'Not so fast, young lady,' he said.

She gave him a challenging look. 'What are you going to do, Alessandro? Call your lawyers and make me pay up?'

His fingers tightened on her arm. 'Go on. Do it. Walk out right now and see what happens. I dare you.'

Her eyes warred with his. 'You want me to break the contract, don't you? You want to prove how unreliable I am. But I'm not leaving until the time is officially up.'

'Then let's not waste any more time of it bickering,' he said, and brought his mouth down with crushing pressure against hers.

Rachel wished she had the strength to resist him but as soon as his lips met hers she was on fire. It had been simmering between them all evening. Her frustration at him continually locking himself away had niggled at her until she had pushed and pushed for a reaction. Now that she had it she wasn't quite sure what to do with it. His response to her was so breathtaking. His erection pressed against her, igniting her desire for him like a match to tinder. He pulled down the bodice of her dress, his mouth covering first one breast and then the other, sucking, biting, drawing on her until she was writhing with need. Her dress slipped to the floor at her feet and she stepped out of it, standing before him in nothing but her high heels and lacy knickers.

He raked her all over with his gaze, the scorching heat of it making her need of him all the more irresistible. 'I want you any way I can have you,' he said in a low rough tone. 'No woman has ever made me want to lose control the way you do.'

Rachel tugged at his bow tie, ripping it out of the collar of his shirt and tossing it to the floor at their feet. She fumbled with the buttons of his dress shirt but with his help she finally managed to get him out of it. She went for his belt and trouser fastenings, her hands greedy for the feel of him against her skin.

He pulled her knickers roughly to one side, and, putting a hand up against the wall near her head to anchor himself, he plunged into her wet softness. She gasped out loud as he filled her; the driving strength and thickness of him almost making her come right then and there. He delved between their hard pressed bodies to pleasure her with his fingers, his magic touch triggering a monumental explosion of ecstasy. She quivered and shook with the earthquake of feeling that rattled through her. He sucked in a harsh breath and then let himself go, the quick hard thrusts releasing the essence of him into the warm cave of her still trembling body.

Alessandro was breathing hard as he looked at her. 'I hope I wasn't too rough with you,' he said.

'Did you hear me complaining?' Rachel said, running a fingertip from his chest to his belly button and back again.

'You're an amazing lover, Rachel,' he said. 'I can't think of a time when I have felt so…so…'

'So lost for words?' Rachel said.

He gave her a rueful smile. 'Yes, that's probably the best way to describe it. You leave me breathless and speechless.'

She played with his chest hair with her fingers, her eyes lowered from his. 'You made me angry.'

'You made me pretty angry too.'

She looked up at him entreatingly. 'I don't want to fight with you.'

He pressed a kiss to her forehead. 'Then let's not fight.'

'So, if we're not going to fight what are we going to do for the rest of the week in Paris?' she asked.

He kissed the side of her neck, his breath feathering over her skin, making her shiver in response. 'I have some meetings with the sheikh but we have most of the week to ourselves.'

She tilted her head to look up at him. 'What do you normally do with your lovers when you come to Paris?'

He frowned at her. 'Why on earth do you want to know that?'

She gave a little shrug. 'Just interested, I guess.'

'Interested or jealous?' he asked.

Rachel held his probing look. 'I don't want to do the same things or go to the same places,' she said. 'I want this time together to be different. I want you to think back to this week in the years to come and not have to ponder on who it was with you when you saw such and such, or ate at such and such a restaurant. I want you to remember it was me and only me.'

'Believe me, *cara*,' he said as he brought his mouth down to hers. 'I will always remember it was you.'

CHAPTER TEN

THE week they spent together in Paris was unforgettable. Rachel knew she would think back on it for the rest of her life as a precious time when she and Alessandro put their differences aside and were just a normal couple exploring the city and surrounds. Alessandro could walk longer and longer distances, but he still relied on his stick, particularly at the end of the day when his muscles became tired. There was no climbing of the Eiffel Tower or spending hours wandering around in the Louvre, but Rachel didn't mind at all. It was enough that she was alone with him, to spend time getting to know him in a way she hadn't been able to before.

At night they avoided the main dining areas and instead ate in small intimate restaurants that had a homely feel. During the day they took car trips to places such as Giverny to see Monet's garden and out to Normandy to visit the abbey of Mont Saint Michel. They stopped at local farms to buy raspberries and sat on a picnic blanket in the countryside feeding them to each other, laughing about their stained fingers or clothes. They drank wine and champagne and ate a different type of cheese every day.

They made love with such passion Rachel's body hummed for hours afterwards. She fell more and more in love with him in spite of the clock ticking on their relationship. She couldn't help it. He made her feel so alive and vibrant. He made her feel as if she was the only woman in the world who could make him complete.

But he didn't say anything about loving her back.

Rachel woke first on the morning of their last day in Paris. She looked at Alessandro while he slept, drinking in his dark arresting features, touching him with a feather-light fingertip, over his eyebrows, down his nose, on his top lip and then his bottom one. Why wouldn't he use that mouth to say the words she most wanted to hear? Her need to hear him say it out loud was like a gnawing ache inside her. It had become almost like an obsession. She thought about it all the time, anticipating the moment when he would finally confess his true feelings.

Alessandro opened his eyes and sent her a lazy smile. 'I was having the most amazing dream,' he said.

Rachel smiled back as she traced his top lip again. 'Tell me about it.'

He rolled her onto her back and looked at her smoulderingly. 'I dreamt I was in bed in a Paris hotel with the most beautiful woman in the world.'

She shivered with delight when his hard body brushed against her softer curves. 'Were you by any chance as madly and hopelessly in love with her as she was with you?' she asked with a playful smile.

His expression froze for a tiny moment but it was enough to shatter the sensual spell. 'Rachel,' he began. 'This has been a crazy week, a crazy couple of weeks, actually. But this is not the real world.'

Rachel felt her stomach sink in disappointment. 'You don't believe I love you, do you? You think I'm only saying it because of the money.'

'I know it's not about the money,' he said as he rose from the bed. 'I know you think you're in love with me. You're confusing physical feelings with emotional ones.'

'At least I have emotional ones,' she threw back resentfully.

He held her gaze for a steely moment before he turned away. 'I have to get ready for my final meeting with the sheikh,' he said. 'I'll call you when I'm through.'

When Alessandro came back from his meeting he announced the deal was completed. His mission had been accomplished, but instead of seeming happy about it he seemed to retreat further into himself as the day went on. He frowned more than he smiled, and was silent more than he talked. His limp seemed to be more pronounced and she saw him wince once or twice when he thought she wasn't looking.

'Is everything all right?' she asked when he stumbled slightly as they walked back to the car after a stop for afternoon tea.

'Of course,' he said.

'I'm sorry about this morning,' she said after another moment. 'I didn't mean that about you being without emotion.'

He glanced at her without speaking, his lips moving in a quick on-off smile.

'You don't seem yourself,' she said after they had driven for a couple of kilometres. 'Yesterday you talked to me the whole way back to the hotel. Today you've said nothing.'

'I'm fine, Rachel,' he said, letting out a relieved sigh. 'It's been a big week. I'm just glad it's over.'

Was he glad their time was drawing to a close? she wondered. There was only a week left. Was he counting down the days now his deal was secure? He hadn't said anything about extending her time with him. She had longed for him to do so. She had longed for him to say he cared about her. That their relationship was not just a business deal, but much, much more. She longed to hear him say he loved her the way she so passionately loved him. She had given him the perfect opportunity to say it but he had deflected yet again.

His silence made her want to press him, to goad him into admitting he wanted her, not just for now, but for ever. 'I'm glad it's over too,' she said, patting her overfull stomach. 'Just as well I'm going home at the end of next week. With all that wining and dining we've done lately, if I were to stay any longer with you I'd get horribly fat.'

He didn't respond and when she looked at him he was frowning yet again.

'Who will you get to take my place?' Rachel asked, not quite able to refrain from intensifying her own torture.

He threw her a dark look. 'What?'

'You know, your next mistress,' she said. 'Have you anyone in mind?'

'Of course not,' he said, his hands like claws on the steering wheel.

'So how do you choose your next mistress?' she asked.

'How does anyone choose a new lover?' he countered. 'It's a matter of chemistry.'

'You can't be such a great judge of chemistry if after a month it always fizzles out,' she said drily.

'Maybe I haven't met the right one just yet,' he said and pulled into the hotel arrivals bay.

The hotel parking attendant took the keys from Alessandro. Rachel was let out of the car by another attendant and joined Alessandro as they walked into the foyer. He was leaning heavily on his stick and his mouth had white tips at the edges as if he was in pain.

'Are you sure you're all right?' Rachel asked.

'I'm fine.'

'You don't look fine,' she said. 'Maybe we should call a doctor.'

'I do not need a doctor,' he snapped at her. 'Now will you stop fussing? You're acting like a wife, not a mistress. It's not what I am paying you to do.'

They travelled in the lift up to their room in a silence that throbbed with tension.

Inside their suite Rachel dumped her bag on one of the sofas and kicked off her shoes. 'I'm going to take a shower,' she said crisply.

'Rachel.'

It was amazing how the way he said her name always made her stop in her tracks. But this time there was a quality to his voice she hadn't heard in it before. A blossoming hope rose in her chest that the reason he had been distancing himself all day was because he was finally working himself up to the confession of love she so longed for. No wonder he was so tense and on edge. He was finding it hard to put his pride to one side and admit he loved and needed her. How sweet, she thought. He was nervous about revealing himself to her. He had purposely waited until his business deal was out of the way before he told her. She slowly turned around to look at him with a soft smile. 'Yes?'

'I have something for you,' he said, handing her a flat jeweller's box he had taken from the dresser next to the bed.

She took it with an unsteady hand, her heart thumping like a wild thing in her chest. 'What is it?'

'Open it,' he said.

Rachel took the box and opened it to find a heavily encrusted diamond and emerald evening necklace with matching dangling earrings. It was beautiful but its showy splendour was not quite to her taste, although she could only imagine how much it must have cost. She wondered if there was something significant about him selecting it for her. 'I'm not sure what to say…' she said. 'It's beautiful but…'

'If you don't like it I can easily get my secretary to choose something else,' he said, releasing his tie as he faced the mirror.

Rachel felt a rod of anger straighten her spine. 'You got your secretary to choose this?'

'Of course,' he said as he faced her. 'She selects all of my gifts.'

Rachel shut the box with a snap and handed it to him. 'I don't want it,' she said.

He frowned at her. 'Rachel, that set is worth more than I've spent on any other lover.'

She glared at him furiously. 'Do you think I care about that? Here, take it back. *Now.*'

He folded his arms to thwart her. 'You could always sell it when our affair is over,' he said. 'Think of it as one of the perks of the job.'

Rachel wanted to slap him but instead she threw the jeweller's box on the bed and stalked to the other side of the room. 'Take it out of my sight,' she said stiffly.

'I really don't know what all the fuss is about,' Alessandro said.

She swung around to look at him. 'How can you say that? *How can you?* I gave you my love for free and now you have cheapened it by buying the most ridiculously expensive jewellery possible. Do you have any idea of how that makes me feel?'

He picked up the box and put it back in the drawer. 'There, the nasty diamonds and emeralds are out of sight. Satisfied now?'

She gave him a fulminating glare. 'How can you do this?'

'Do what?' he asked with a snap of his brows.

'You made love to me all week, treating me like a princess, and then you pay me off with a shabby box of jewellery you didn't even take the time and effort to choose yourself,' she said.

'Five years ago I gave you a piece of jewellery I chose myself and you threw it back in my face and took another man's ring instead,' he said with a sneering curl of his lip. 'Why would I take the time and effort to go through all that again?'

The air pulsated with bitterness.

Rachel took a breath that scalded her throat. 'I can't do this any longer,' she said. 'I don't care if you throw me to your greedy lawyers to be eaten up alive. I can't be with you any more, not even for another week, not even for another day, not even for another hour.'

His expression turned to stone. 'You will have to deal with the consequences if you leave now.'

She swallowed as she thought of Caitlyn and the team back home. Would he do it? Would he destroy her to have his final revenge? It was a risk she had to take. 'Do whatever you think you should do,' she said, turning away in case he saw the heart-wrenching despair in her gaze.

When Rachel had packed her things and come out he was leaning against the bar with a drink in his hand. From the slight flush high on his cheeks it hadn't been the first drink he had consumed in her short absence.

'I'm going now,' she announced.

'Fine.' He raised his shot glass and drained it, putting it down on the bar again with a snap.

'Aren't you going to see me out?'

'I think you can find the door on your own.'

Rachel felt her heart go into a painful spasm. 'It doesn't have to be this way.'

He refilled his glass. 'Yes, it does.'

'You could stop me from leaving with a word,' she said.

'I don't want you to stay,' he said, addressing his empty glass. 'It's over, Rachel. I should never have started it. It was a moment of madness.'

A silence fell like a curtain.

'Will you say goodbye to Lucia for me?' Rachel said when she could get her voice to work without breaking.

'Of course,' he said. 'She will be very sad to see you go. She liked you. She liked you a lot.'

'I liked her too,' Rachel said. She waited for a moment but his back was still stiffly turned against her. 'Goodbye, then. I probably won't see you again.'

'No,' he said, refilling his glass.

Alessandro waited until the door closed on her exit before he pushed the untouched drink away. He wanted to chase after her and beg her to stay but how could he tie her to him now? It was better this way. She would move on with her life soon enough. He didn't want to see her looking at him with pity. He could bear anything but that. 'Damn it,' he said dropping his head into his hands. 'Damn it to hell.'

It was four weeks before he was back on his feet and even then it was with a limp that his specialist had hinted might be permanent. Alessandro had not anticipated a relapse but apparently it was a feature of Guillain-Barré syndrome. He vaguely remembered being informed of that the first time but he had dismissed it out of hand. He had absolutely refused to accept it as a possibility. He hadn't for a moment contemplated not returning to full health and mobility. He had only focused on getting well. He had worked so hard to regain his strength. Weeks and weeks of physical therapy and after that week in Paris he had gone back to square one. But he was finally getting better and the time in rehab had taught him much more than accepting his limitations.

Rachel had once pointed out to him that his life was full of success but no happiness. Even Sheikh Almeed Khaled on a surprise visit to the hospital had reiterated what he had said about her being perfect for him, that the love she felt for him was a rare thing and should be treasured. It had made Alessandro realise that love should not have conditions attached. The greatest gift he had ever been given was Rachel's love and he had turned it down out of fear.

The flight to Melbourne had been arduous irrespective of the private jet he had organised. He wanted to see Rachel and he would not be able to rest until he did. He hoped she hadn't hooked up with someone else. He hoped her feelings for him were genuine, that in spite of everything she would take him back. He had never felt so insecure and vulnerable before but he could not get on with his life without knowing if Rachel wanted him with all his faults and failings.

He stood outside the building that housed her label. At least he had been able to save that for her. Her designs had attracted a lot of interest over the last few weeks. A major department store had signed her up for an exclusive showing that would open up other doors for her both here and in Europe.

A model-thin young woman blinked owlishly at him from behind the counter. 'Can I help you?' she said.

'I was hoping to see Rachel,' he said. 'I'm an…an old friend.'

'I'm sorry,' the girl said. 'But Rachel has gone home sick.'

Alessandro frowned. 'Is she all right?'

'I don't know,' the girl said. 'That's the third day in a row she's left early. Must be a stomach bug or something. She hasn't been well since she got back from Italy.'

Alessandro took the address the girl had scribbled down for him. He closed his fist over it and limped to where his hire car was parked. He knew he should probably phone first but he wanted to see her so badly he didn't want to waste time. He got behind the wheel and drove to her suburb, parking outside the modest apartment with his heart lodged in his throat. Would she agree to see him or slam the door in his face? He patted his pocket where he had put the ring he'd had specially designed for her. Would it be enough to convince her he wanted her in his life for ever?

She opened the door after what seemed a very long time. Alessandro felt his chest cramp at the sight of her. She looked as if she hadn't slept in the whole time they had been apart. Her eyes were underscored with shadows that looked like thumb-print bruises and her skin looked deathly pale.

'Alessandro…' she said, her colour fading even more. 'What are you doing here?'

'I wanted to see you.'

'Um… Now's not such a great time,' she said, looking back over her shoulder nervously.

Alessandro felt a pain unlike any he had felt before. 'Just five minutes,' he said. 'Surely you can give me that?'

She pressed her lips together. 'I'm busy right now.'

'I can wait.'

She looked at him with a stricken expression. 'You have to go away and come back some other time.'

'I'm not leaving,' he said implacably. 'I should never have let you go the way I did. I spent almost a month in hospital berating myself for letting you go.'

Her eyes rounded in shock. 'You were in hospital?'

'I was admitted the night you left.'

Her face fell. 'Why didn't you tell me? I asked and asked but you insisted everything was fine.'

'I didn't want you to feel obligated,' he said. 'It seemed wiser to let you go.'

She looked at him in frustration. 'Do you have any idea of how much you hurt me?'

'I know and I'm sorry.' He took out the ring box. 'I have something for you.'

She rolled her eyes. 'Tell your secretary to enrol in some taste classes.'

'My secretary had nothing to do with it,' he said, handing her the box. 'I designed it myself.'

Rachel opened the velvet box to see a brilliant diamond sparkling there. 'You designed this?'

'Do you like it?'

She ran her fingertip over the exquisite setting. 'It's beautiful.'

'It's an engagement ring,' Alessandro said, 'just in case you hadn't noticed.'

She looked up at him. 'You're asking me to marry you?'

'Yes,' he said. 'Will you?'

Rachel handed him back the ring. 'I need some time to think about it.'

Alessandro swallowed tightly. 'Don't do this to me, Rachel, even if I deserve it.'

'You won't say it, will you?' she asked, her eyes misting over.

He suddenly realised the step he had overlooked. '*Cara*, I love you,' he said. 'I love you more than words can say, which is probably why I find it so hard to say it in words. But it's true. I love you. I loved you five years ago and I love you now.'

Her expression brightened with joy. 'You really mean it?'

He brought her close. 'Yes, but I think you should know something from the outset,' he said. 'I'm probably always going to have this wretched limp.'

She gave a shrug. 'So what? I can walk and run for both of us.'

'I also have a business in Italy that I can't leave,' he added.

'I have a business that is in need of an Italian outlet,' she said. 'I can leave Caitlyn in charge of this end of things and base myself in Italy. It's a perfect solution.'

His brow furrowed. 'You'd do that for me?'

She smiled at him. 'I would do anything for you. Don't you realise that by now?'

Alessandro touched her face, hardly able to believe what he was hearing. 'I have wanted you for so long. I didn't realise how much I loved you until Sheikh Almeed Khaled told me how perfect you were for me at that dinner we had that night.'

Rachel's expression brightened. 'He said that?'

'Yes, but I panicked,' he said. 'I kept trying to hold you aloft all that week, reminding you of that stupid contract whenever I could, hoping you wouldn't see how much I loved and needed you.'

She looked back at him with shining eyes. 'You really don't hate me for what I did when I chose Craig instead of you?'

He brushed his thumb against her bottom lip. 'I thought I did for a time, but just lately I have realised how I misjudged you. You tried so hard to do the right thing. You gave up your own happiness to please your father. He was the one who warned the financial backers about you, by the way.'

Rachel frowned in dismay. '*He* did that?'

Alessandro cupped her cheek. 'Yes, but not for the reasons you think,' he said. 'I called him about it a couple of weeks ago to confirm it. Right from the start I suspected it might have been him. He wanted you to come to me for help. It was his way of atoning for what he had done by insisting you accept Hughson's proposal.'

Rachel was astonished. 'He *wanted* me to come to you?'

He gave her a rueful look. 'I was wrong about him too, *cara*,' he said. 'He does want you to be happy and successful, but even more than that he wants you to have a happy marriage. And children too, at least two, or three.'

Rachel swallowed. 'Did you say…*children*?'

Alessandro smiled. 'What's the point of having all this success if you have no one to share it with?'

'But I thought—'

He put his finger across her lips. 'I want what you want, *tesoro mio*,' he said. 'I want it all: marriage and babies and happy ever after. How soon do you think we can get going on the baby thing?'

Rachel smiled radiantly as she slid her hands around his neck. 'There's something waiting in the bathroom that should tell us one way or the other on that. That's what I was doing when you came. I think the three minutes is up by now.'

His eyes melted as they held hers. 'You're pregnant?'

'I don't know,' she said, squeezing his hands in excitement. 'Shall we go upstairs and see?'

EPILOGUE

As it turned out Rachel missed her much anticipated debut at the Milan Fashion Show but she wasn't one bit disappointed. She looked up at Alessandro after the safe arrival of baby Leonardo Tristano Vallini. 'Not bad for a first effort, don't you think?' she said with a tired but happy smile.

Alessandro was still unashamedly wiping away tears from his eyes as he cradled his infant son. 'Stupendous, *cara*,' he said. 'But then everything you do is magic.'

Rachel leaned against him in blissful satisfaction. Their life together was about as perfect as she had hoped. Alessandro had made a steady recovery, and his limp was hardly noticeable, or so she insisted. Their wedding day had been a romantic and emotional event that people were still talking about all over Europe. Rachel had designed her own dress and the buzz about it had kick-started her wedding design branch of the label in Italy. Her father had flown over with his new partner Jane, a no-nonsense, steady type of woman who brought out the best in him. Rachel had never seen her father so settled and happy and because of his happiness he was able to be a much better father than he had ever been before.

'Are you very disappointed about missing your first fashion show?' Alessandro asked, gently brushing back the damp strands of hair off her forehead with his free hand.

Rachel looked up at his loving expression. 'No,' she said. 'Caitlyn will tell me all about it later. This is much more important: being a family for the first time.'

'A family…' 'Alessandro's voice cracked over the words. 'I never thought I would ever have one of my own. You have made me such a happy man, *cara mio*. Do you have any idea of how much I love you?'

She smiled at him with tears of happiness in her eyes. 'I think I'm getting used to the fact, but just to be sure you probably should tell me every day for the next fifty or so years. Is it a deal?'

He leaned down and kissed her soundly. 'It's a deal.'

* * * * *

A sneaky peek at next month...

MODERN™

INTERNATIONAL AFFAIRS, SEDUCTION & PASSION GUARANTEED

My wish list for next month's titles...

In stores from 16th September 2011:

☐ The Most Coveted Prize – Penny Jordan

☐ The Night that Changed Everything – Anne McAllister

☐ The Lost Wife – Maggie Cox

☐ Weight of the Crown – Christina Hollis

☐ Bought: His Temporary Fiancée – Yvonne Lindsay

In stores from 7th October 2011:

☐ The Costarella Conquest – Emma Darcy

☐ Craving the Forbidden – India Grey

☐ Heiress Behind the Headlines – Caitlin Crews

☐ Innocent in the Ivory Tower – Lucy Ellis

Available at WHSmith, Tesco, Asda, Eason, Amazon and Apple

Just can't wait?

Visit us Online

You can buy our books online a month before they hit the shops! **www.millsandboon.co.uk**

0911/01

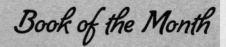

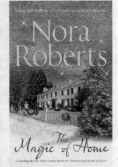

Have Your Say

You've just finished your book.
So what did you think?

We'd love to hear your thoughts on our
'Have your say' online panel
www.millsandboon.co.uk/haveyoursay

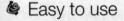

- Easy to use
- Short questionnaire
- Chance to win Mills & Boon®
  goodies

Visit us
Online
Tell us what you thought of this book now at
www.millsandboon.co.uk/haveyoursay

YOUR_SAY

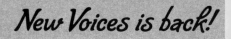